THE MYSTICS

MORE WILDSIDE CLASSICS

THE MYSTICS

KATHERINE CECIL THURSTON

WILDSIDE PRESS

THE MYSTICS

This edition published in 2007 by Wildside Press, LLC.
www.wildsidebooks.com

CHAPTER I

Of all the sensations to which the human mind is a prey, there is none so powerful in its finality, so chilling in its sense of an impending event as the knowledge that Death — grim, implacable Death — has cast his shadow on a life that custom and circumstance have rendered familiar. Whatever the personal feeling may be — whether dismay, despair, or relief — no man or woman can watch that advancing shadow without a quailing at the heart, an individual shrinking from the terrible, natural mystery that we must all face in turn — each for himself and each alone.

In a gaunt house on the loneliest point where the Scottish coast overlooks the Irish Sea, John Henderson was watching his uncle die. In the plain, whitewashed room where the sick man lay, a fire was burning and a couple of oil-lamps shed an uncertain glow; but outside, the wind roared inland from the shore, and the rain splashed in furious showers against the windows of the house. It was a night of tumult and darkness; but neither the old man who lay waiting for the end nor the young man who watched that end approaching gave any heed to the turmoil of the elements. Each was self-engrossed.

Except for an occasional rasping cough, or a slow, indrawn breath, no sign came from the small iron bedstead on which the dying man lay. His hard, emaciated face was set in an impenetrable mask; his glazed eyes were fixed immovably on a distant portion of the ceiling; and his hands lay clasped upon his breast, covering some object that depended from his neck.

He had lain thus since the doctor from the neighboring town had braved the rising storm and ridden over to see him in the fall of the evening; and no accentuation of the gale that lashed the house, no increase in the roar of the ocean three hundred yards away, had power to interrupt his lethargy.

In curious contrast was the expression that marked his nephew's face. An extraordinary suppressed energy was visible in every line of John Henderson's body as he sat crouching over the fire; and a look of irrepressible excitement smoldered in the eyes that gazed into the glowing coals. He was barely twenty-three years old, but the self-control that comes from endurance and privation sat unmistakably on his knitted brows and closed lips. He was neither handsome of feature nor graceful of figure, yet there was something more striking and interesting than either grace or beauty in the strong, youthful form and the strong, intelligent face. For a long time he retained his crouching seat on the wooden stool that stood before the hearth; then at last the activity at work within his mind made further inaction intolerable. He rose and turned towards the bed.

The dying man lay motionless, awaiting the final summons with that aloofness that suggests a spirit already partially extricated from its covering of flesh. His glassy eyes were still fixed and immovable save for an occasional twitching of the eyelids; his pallid lips were drawn back from his strong, prominent teeth; and the skin about his temples looked shrivelled and sallow. The doctor's parting words came sharply to the younger man's mind.

"Sit still and watch him — you can do no more."

He reiterated this injunction many times mentally as he stood contemplating the man who for seven interminable years had ruled, repressed, and worked him as he might have worked a well-constructed, manageable machine; and a sudden rush of joy, of freedom and recompense flooded his heart and set his pulses throbbing. He momentarily lost sight of the grim shadow hovering over the house. The sense of emancipation rose tumultuously, over-ruling even the immense solemnity of approaching Death.

John Henderson had known little of the easy, pleasant paths of life, carpeted by wealth and sheltered by influence. His most childish and distant recollections carried him back to days of anxious poverty. His father, the elder son of a wealthy Scottish landowner, had quarrelled with his father, and at the age of twenty left his home, disinherited in favor of his younger brother. Possessed of a peculiar temperament — passionate, headstrong, dogged in his resolves, he had shaken the dust of Scotland from his feet; sworn never to be beholden to either father or brother for the fraction of a penny, and had gone out into the world to seek his fortune. But the fortune had been far to seek. For years he had followed the sea; for years he had toiled on land; but in every under-taking failure stalked him. Finally, at the age of fifty, he touched success for the first time. He fell in love and found his love returned. But here again the irony of fate was constant in its pur-suit. The object of his choice was the daughter of an artist, a man as needy, as entirely unfortunate as he himself.

But love at fifty is sometimes as blind as love at twenty-five. With an improvidence that belied his nationality, Alick Hen-derson married after a courtship as brief as it was happy. For a year he shared the hap-hazard life of his wife and father-in-law; then Nature saw fit to alter the small *ménage*. The artist died, and almost at the same time little John was born.

With the coming of the child, Henderson conceived a new impetus and also a new sense of bitterness and self-reproach. A homeless failure may tramp the face of the earth and feel no shame; but the unsuccessful man who is a husband and a father moves upon a different plane. He has ties — responsibilities — something for which he must answer to himself.

There is pathos in the picture of a man setting forth at fifty-one to conquer the world anew; and its grim futility is not good to look upon. Henderson had failed for himself, and he failed equal-ly for others. The years that followed his marriage were but the unwinding of a pitifully old story. Before his boy was ten years old he had run the gamut of humiliation; he had done everything that the pinch of poverty could demand, except apply for aid to his brother Andrew. This even the faithful, patient wife who had stood stanch in all his trials never dared to suggest.

In this atmosphere John learned to look upon life. A naturally high-spirited and courageous child, he gradually fell under that spell of premature understanding that is the portion of a mind forced too soon to realize the significance of ways and means. Day by day his serious eyes grew to comprehend the lines that marked his mother's beloved face; to know the cost at which his own edu-cation, his own wants, were supplied by the tired, silent father, who, despite his shabby clothes and prematurely broken air, seemed perpetually to move in the glamour of a past romance; and gradually, steadily, passionately, as these things came home to him, there grew up in his youthful mind a desire to compensate by his own future for the struggle he daily witnessed.

Many were the nights when — his lessons for the next day finished, and his father away at one of the many precarious tasks that kept the household together — he would draw close to his mother, as she sat industriously sewing, and beg her for the hundredth time to recount the story of the grim Scotch home where his father had lost his birthright; of the stern old grandfather who had died inexorably unforgiving; of the unknown uncle of whom rumor told many eccentric stories. And, roused by the recital, his boyish face would flush, his boyish mind leap forward towards the future.

"'Twill all come back, mother!" he would cry. "'Twill all come back! I'll win it back!"

And, with a sobbing laugh, his mother would drop her sewing and draw him to her heart in a sudden yearning of love and pride.

In such surroundings and in such an atmosphere he passed sixteen years; then the first upheaval of his life took place. His father died.

His first recollection — when the terrible necessities of the event were past, and his own grief and consternation had partially subsided — was the remembrance of his mother calling him to her room; of her kissing him, crying over him and telling him of the resolve she had taken to write and make known his existence to his uncle in Scotland.

The confession at first overwhelmed him. His own pride, his sense of loyalty to his father's memory prompted him to cry out against the idea as against a sacrilege. Then slowly his boyish, immature mind grasped something of the nobility that prompted the decision — something of the inexpressible love that counted sentiment and personal dignity as nothing beside his own future; and in a passion of gratitude he flung his arms about his mother, repeating the old childish vows with a new and deeper force.

So the letter to Scotland was despatched; and a time of sharp suspense followed for mother and son. Then, one never-to-be-forgotten day, the answer arrived.

Andrew Henderson wrote unemotionally. He expressed formal regret for his brother's death, but evinced no interest in his sister-in-law's position. He briefly described himself as living an isolated life in a small house on the sea-coast, a dozen miles from the family home which had remained untenanted since his father's death. He admitted that with advancing years the duties of life had begun to weigh upon him, diverting his mind and time from the graver pursuits to which his life was devoted; finally he grudgingly suggested that, should his nephew care to undertake the duties of secretary at a salary of sixty pounds a year, he might find a home with him.

The immediate feeling that followed the reading of the letter was fraught with chilling disappointment. On the moment, pride again asserted itself, urging a swift refusal of the rich man's proposal; then once more the patience that had kept Mrs. Henderson brave and gentle during seventeen years of wearing poverty made itself felt. All thought of personal grievance faded from her mind as she pointed out the urgent necessity of John's being seen and known by this uncle, whose only relation and ostensible heir he was. She talked for long, wisely and kindly — as mothers talk out of the unselfish fulness of their hearts — and with every word the golden castles of her imagination rose tower on tower to form the citadel in which her son was to reign supreme.

So wisely and so lovingly did she talk that she persuaded not only the boy, but herself, into the belief that he had but to reach Scotland to make his inheritance sure; and before the day closed she wrote to Andrew Henderson accepting his offer. A week later the whole light of her life went out, as she watched the train steam out of the station, carrying John northward.

Upon the days that followed his arrival in Scotland there is no need to dwell. He came as a stranger, and as a stranger he was introduced by his uncle to the routine of work expected of him. No mention was made of his recent loss, no suggestion was given that his mother should make her double bereavement easier by visits to her son. Whatever of hope or sentiment he had brought with him, he was left to destroy or smother as best he could.

The first week resolved itself into one round of boyish homesickness and desolation; then gradually, as the marvellous healing properties of youth began to stir, a new feeling awakened in his mind — a sense of curiosity concerning the strange old man whom fate, by a twist of the wheel, had made the arbiter of his life. Even to one so young and inexperienced, it was impossible to know Andrew Henderson and not to feel that some strange peculiarity set him apart from other men. In his ascetic face, in his large, light-blue eyes, in his extraordinary air of abstraction and aloofness from mundane things, there was something that fascinated and repelled; and with a wondering interest the boy studied these things, trying in his unformed way to reconcile them with his narrow experience of human nature.

For many weeks he sought without success for some key to the attitude of this new-found relative. Then one evening — when solution seemed least near — the key, metaphorically speaking, fell at his feet. Returning home from a ramble over the headland, his observant eye was caught by the sight of a narrow foot-track that, crossing the main pathway of the cliff, wound steeply upward and seemingly lost itself in a tangle of gorse and bracken. Stirred by a boyish desire for exploration, he paused, turned into this obscure track, and incontinently began its ascent.

For some hundreds of yards it led upward in a sharp incline; and with its added steepness, the ardor of the explorer warmed. With impetuous haste he climbed the last dozen yards; when, as the anticipated summit was reached, he halted in abrupt, dismayed surprise; for with alarming suddenness the land broke off short, disclosing a deep gap or fissure, carpeted with heather and surrounded by natural protecting walls of rock, in the centre of which was set a miniature chapel built of dark stone.

At sight of the little edifice, he thrilled with adventurous surprise. There was something mysterious, something almost fine in the sight of the small temple, with the setting sun gleaming on its solid walls, its low, massive door and round window of thick stained glass. He leaned out over the shelving rock, staring down upon it with wide, astonished eyes; then the natural instinct of the boy overtopped every other feeling. With a quick-movement of excitement and expectation, he began to descend into the hollow.

But though he walked round the little building a dozen times, shook the heavy door and peered ineffectually into the opaque window, nothing rewarded his curiosity, and after half an hour of diligent endeavor he was compelled to return home no wiser than when he had first stood on the summit of the path and looked down into the rocky cleft.

All that evening, however, the thought of his discovery remained with him. At the eight-o'clock supper of porridge, vegetables, and fruit which he shared with his uncle, he chafed under the silence of his companion and at the air of calm indifference that the whitewashed room with its raftered ceiling seemed to wear; and it was with a sigh of satisfaction that he rose from table and bade his uncle a formal good-night.

With the same suggestion of relief, he watched the old man light his candle and ascend the bare stairs to his own room; then prompted by the impulse he never neglected, he went into the study to write the daily letter that made his mother's existence bearable.

He wrote for nearly an hour, omitting no detail of the evening's discovery. Then, as he closed and sealed the letter, a clock on the mantel-piece struck ten. The sound had an oddly hollow and chilly effect in the bare, carpetless room; and unconsciously he raised his head and glanced about him. His ideas, still stirred by his adventure, were more prone than usual to the suggestion of outward things; and for almost the first time since his arrival, he felt drawn to study his intimate surroundings. With a new curiosity he let his eyes wander from the severe book-shelves to the ugly iron safe that stood in the most prominent position in the room; and from the safe his glance turned to the revolving book-case by his uncle's favorite chair, in which lay the volumes that were in daily use. Following an impulse he had never previously been conscious of, he crossed the room, and drawing three books, at hap-hazard from the case, studied their titles.

The Indissoluble Essence, he read; *The Soul in Relation to the Human Mind*; *The Mystic Influence*.

He stood for a space gazing at the sombre covers, but making no attempt to dip into their pages; then a sudden look of comprehension sprang into his eyes. The oddly built stone chapel took on a new and more personal meaning. With a quick gesture he thrust the books back into their place, extinguished the lamp, and softly left the room. Gaining the hall, he did not turn towards the stairs; but tiptoeing to the table, picked up his cap, crossed the hall noiselessly and opened the outer door.

The warmth of the August day was still heavy on the air as he stepped into the open; a great copper-colored moon hung low over the sea, and a soft, filmy haze lay over both land and water. Without hesitation he turned into the cliff path, and followed it until his quick eyes caught the indistinct foot-track that he had discovered earlier in the evening. With the same decision, the same suggestion of anticipation, he stepped rapidly forward and once more began the sharp ascent.

The impetus of his curiosity carried him forward; he mounted the path in hot haste; then, as he gained the summit, he halted again, but in new surprise. In the hazy, mellow moonlight, the small building stood out sharp and dark as on his previous visit, but from the round, stained-glass window a flood of light — crimson, rose-color, and gold — poured out into the night.

CHAPTER II

In the first moment of astonishment, John stood motionless, his gaze riveted on the glow of color that poured through the window upon the rocks and heather of the cleft. Then, as he continued to stand with widely opened eyes, another surprise was sprung upon him. The door of the chapel opened and the figure of his uncle — long since supposed to be sleeping tranquilly in his own room — showed tall and angular in the aperture.

From John's position, the open door and the lighted interior of the little edifice were distinctly visible; and in one glance he saw his uncle's silhouetted figure and behind it a bare space some dozen feet square, lined on floor and walls with sections of marble alternately black and white. From the ceiling of this chamber depended an octagonal symbol in polished metal, and close by the door eight wax candles flickered slightly in the faint stir of air. But his astonished and inquisitive eyes had barely become aware of these details when Andrew Henderson turned towards the circular sconce in which the candles were set and began to extinguish them one by one. As the light died, he stepped forward and John drew back sharply; but at his movement a stone, loosened by his heel, went rolling down into the hollow. And a moment later his uncle, glancing up, saw his figure outlined against the luminous sky.

What the outcome of the incident would have been on any other occasion, it is difficult to say. As it was, the moment was propitious. Old Henderson, surprised in an instant of exaltation, was pleased to put his own narrow, superstitious construction on the boy's appearance. Laboring under an abnormal excitement, he showed no resentment at the fact of being spied upon; but calling John to him, ordered him to walk home beside him across the cliff.

Never was walk so strange — never were companions so ill-matched as the two who threaded their way back over the headland. Andrew Henderson walked first, talking all the time in a jargon addressed partly to the boy, partly to himself, in which mysticism was oddly tangled with a confusion of crazy theories and beliefs; behind came John, half fascinated and wholly bewildered by the medley of words that poured out upon the night.

On reaching the house, the old man became suddenly silent again, falling back as if by habit into the morose absorption that marked his daily life; but as he turned to mount the stairs to his own room, he paused and his curious light-blue eyes travelled over his nephew's face.

"Good-night!" he said. "You make a good listener."

And John — still confused and silent — retired to bed, to lie awake for many hours, partly thrilled and partly elated by the awesome thought that there was a madman in the house.

*****

But all that had happened seven years ago, and now Andrew Henderson lay waiting for his end. In those seven years John had passed through the mill of deadly monotony that saps even youth, and lulls every instinct save hope. The first enthusiasm of romance that had wrapped the discovery of his uncle's secret had faded out with time. By slow degrees he had learned — partly from his own observation, partly from the old man's occasional fanatic outbursts — that the strange chapel with its metal symbol and marble floor was not the outcome of a private whim, but the manifestation of a creed that boasted a small but ardent band of followers. He had learned that — to themselves, if not to the world — these devotees were known as the Mystics; that their articles of faith were preserved in a secret book designated the Scitsym, which passed in rotation each year from one to another of the six Arch-Mystics, remaining in the care of each for two months out of the twelve. He had discovered that London was the Centre of this sect; and that its fundamental belief was the anticipation of a mysterious prophet — human, and yet divinely inspired — by whose coming the light was to extend from the small and previously unknown band across the whole benighted world.

He had learned all these things. He had been stirred to a passing awe by the discovery that his uncle was, in his own person, actually one of the profound Six who formed the Council of the sect and to whom alone the secrets of its creed were known; and for three successive years his interest and curiosity had been kindled when Andrew Henderson travelled to England and returned with the Arch-Councillor — an old blind man of seventy — who invariably spent one day and night mysteriously closeted with his host and then left, having deposited the sacred Scitsym with his own hands in the tall iron safe that stood in Henderson's study. But that annual excitement had lessened with time. Even a madman may become monotonous when we live with him, day in, day out, for seven long years; and gradually the attitude of John's mind had changed with the passage of time. The sense of adventure and triumphant enterprise had steadily receded; the knowledge that he was working out a slow, distasteful probation had advanced. Reluctantly and yet definitely he had realized that his position was not to come and conquer, but to watch and wait; and this consciousness of a tacitly expected end had grown with the years — with the growth of his mind and body. It was not that he was hard-natured. The regularity with which he despatched his yearly money to his mother — reserving the merest fraction for himself — precluded that idea. But he was young and human, and he was youthfully and humanly greedy to possess the good things of life for himself and for the one being he passionately loved. It would, indeed, have been an enthusiast in virtue who could have blamed him for counting upon dead men's shoes.

And now the shoes were all but empty! He stood watching his uncle die!

Having stayed almost motionless for several minutes, he glanced at the clock; then moved to the bed, taking a bottle and a medicine spoon from the dressing-table as he passed.

"Time for your medicine, uncle!" he said, in his quiet, level voice.

But the sick man did not seem to hear.

In a slightly louder tone John repeated his remark. This time the vacant expression faded slowly from the large, pale eyes, and Andrew Henderson moved his head weakly.

Seeing the indication of consciousness, John carefully measured out a dose of medicine, and, stooping over the pillows, passed one arm under his uncle's neck.

Andrew Henderson submitted without objection, but as his head was raised and the medicine held to his lips, he seemed suddenly to realize the position, to comprehend that it was his nephew who leaned over him. With a spasmodic movement he turned towards John, his lips twitching with some inward and newly aroused excitement.

"The Book, John!" he said, sharply — "the Book!"

John remained quite composed. With a steady hand he balanced the spoon of medicine that he still held.

"Your medicine first, uncle," he said, quietly. "We'll talk about the Book after."

But the old man's calm had been disturbed. With unexpected strength he raised one thin hand and pushed the spoon aside, spilling the contents on the bed.

"How can I leave it?" he exclaimed. "How can I go and leave the Book unguarded?" Again his lips twitched and a feverish brightness flickered in his eyes as they searched his nephew's face.

"When I go, John," he added, excitedly, "the Book may be in your keeping for hours — perhaps for a whole night. I know the Arch-Councillor will answer my summons immediately; but it is possible he may be delayed. It may be the ordination of the Unknown that I should Pass before he arrives. If this is so, I want you to guard the Book — but also I want you to guard my dead body. Let no one touch it until he comes. The key of the safe is here —" He fumbled weakly for the thin chain that hung about his neck. "No one must remove it — no one must touch it until he comes —" His voice faltered.

With a calm gesture John forced him back upon the pillows, and quietly wiped up the medicine.

But with a fresh effort the old man lifted himself again.

"John," he cried, suddenly, "do you understand what I am saying? Do you understand that for a whole night you may be alone with the inviolable Scitsym? 'The Hope of the Universe, by whose Light alone the One and Only Prophet shall be made known unto the Watchers!'" He murmured the quotation in a low, rapt voice.

Again the younger man attempted to soothe him.

"Don't distress yourself!" he said, gravely. "I am here. You can trust me. Lie back and rest."

But his uncle's face was still excitedly perturbed; his pale eyes still possessed an unnatural brightness.

"Oh yes!" he said, sharply, "I trust you! I have trusted you. I have left a letter by which you will see that I have trusted you — and that your fidelity has been rewarded. But this is another matter. Can I trust you in this? Can I trust you as myself?" As he put the question a sweat of weakness and excitement broke out over his forehead.

But it was neither his wild appearance nor his question that suddenly sent the blood into John's face and suddenly set his heart bounding. It was the abrupt and unlooked-for justification of his own secret, treasured hope; the tacit acknowledgment of kinship and obligation made now by Andrew Henderson after seven unfruitful years. A mist rose before his sight and his mind swam. What was the mad creed of a dying man — of a dozen dying men — when the reward of his own long probation awaited him?

But the old man was set to his purpose. With shaking fingers he fumbled with two small objects that depended from the chain about his neck. And as he held them up, John saw by the glow of the lamp that one was a copy in miniature of the metal symbol that decorated the little chapel, the other a long, thin key.

As Henderson disentangled and raised these objects to the light, his eyes turned again upon his nephew.

"John," he said, tremulously, "I want you to swear to me by the Sign that you will not touch my body — nor anything on my body — till the Arch-Councillor comes! Swear, as you hope for your own happiness!" A wild illumination spread over his face; the unpleasant fanatical light showed again in his eyes.

For a moment John looked at him; then stirred by his own emotions, by the new pang of self-reproach and gratitude towards this half-crazy man so near his end, he went forward and touched the small octagonal symbol that gleamed in the light.

"I swear — by the Sign!" he said, in a low, level voice. And almost as the words escaped him, the chain slipped from old Henderson's fingers, his jaw dropped, and his head fell forward on his chest.

The moments that follow an important event are seldom of a nature to be accurately analyzed. For a long while John remained motionless and speechless, unable to realize that the huddled figure still warm in his arms was in reality the vessel of clay from which a spirit had escaped. Then suddenly the realization of the position came to him; with a sharp movement he stood upright, and seizing the bell-rope, pulled it vigorously.

When the old woman who attended to the household appeared, he pointed to her master's body and explained in a few words how the end had come; and how in a last urgent command Henderson had forbidden his body to be touched until the arrival of a member of his religious sect. The old woman accepted the explanation with the apathy common to those who have outlived emotion; and with a series of nods and unintelligible mutterings methodically proceeded to straighten the already neatly arranged furniture of the room, in the instinctive belief that order is the first tribute to be paid to Death.

With something of the same feeling John drew the coverlet over the dead body, then turned to watch the old woman at her work. But as he looked at her a desire to be alone again swept over him, and with the desire a corresponding impatience of her slow and measured movements. Chide himself as he might for his impatience, curb his natural instinct as he might, it was humanly impossible that his strong and eager spirit could give thought to Death — while Life was claiming him with out-stretched hands.

He held himself rigidly in check until the last chair had been arranged and the last cinder swept from the hearth; then as the old woman slowly crossed the room and stepped out into the corridor, he sprang with irrepressible impetuosity and shut and locked the door.

He had no superstitious consciousness of the dead body so close at hand. The dead body — and with it the dead years and the long probation — belonged to the past; he with his youth, his strength, his hope, was bound for the limitless future.

Without a moment's hesitation he crossed to his uncle's bureau, which stood as he had left it three days before when his last illness had seized upon him. The papers were all in order; the ink was as yet scarcely rusted on the pens; the key protruded from the lock of the private drawer. With a tremor of excitement John extended his hand, turned it and opened the drawer; then he caught his breath. There lay a square white envelope addressed to himself in his uncle's fantastic, crooked handwriting.

As he drew it out and held it for a moment in his hand, his thoughts centred unerringly round one object. In a moment, the seven years of waiting — the strange death scene just enacted — even Andrew Henderson and his mystical creed — were blotted from his mind by a wonderful rose-colored mist of hope, from which one face looked out — the patient, tender, pathetic face of the mother he adored. The emotions, so long suppressed, welled up as they had been wont to do years ago in the sordid London home.

With a throb of confidence and anticipation he inserted his finger under the flap of the envelope and tore it open. With lightning speed his eyes skimmed the oddly written lines. Then a short, inarticulate sound escaped him, and the blood suddenly receded from his face.

"MY DEAR NEPHEW," he read. — "In acknowledgment of your services during the past seven years — and also because I have no wish to pass into the Unseen with the stain of vindictiveness on my Soul — I have obliterated from my mind the remembrance of my brother's ingratitude to our father, and have placed the sum of £500 to your credit in the Cleef branch of the Consolidated Bank. I trust it may assist you to commence an industrious career. For the rest, it may interest you to know that my capital, which I realized upon your grandfather's death, is already placed in the treasury of the sect to which I belong — where it will remain until claimed by the One in whose ultimate advent I most solemnly believe.

"I make you cognizant of these facts that all disputes and unnecessary differences may be avoided after my death. The papers by which my property was made over to the Mystics some five years ago — together with a doctor's certificate as to my mental soundness at the time — is in the hands of the Council. Any attempt to unmake this disposition of my fortune would be fraught with failure.

"With sincere hopes for your future welfare,

"Your uncle,

"ANDREW HENDERSON."

For a space John stood pale and rigid, making no attempt to reread the letter; then all at once one of those rare and curious upheavals of feeling that shake men to their souls seized upon him. The blood rushed back into his face in a dark wave; the rose-colored mist that had floated before his vision flamed suddenly to red; the same implacable rage that, years ago, had impelled his grandfather to disinherit his favorite son swelled in his heart. All ideas, all considerations, save one, became blurred and indistinct; but this one idea rode him, spurred him to a frenzy of desire. It was the blind, instinctive, human wish to wreak his loss and disappointment upon some tangible, visible object.

With a dazed movement he turned to the bed; but only the huddled, impassive figure beneath the coverlet met his gaze. For more than a minute he stared at it helplessly; then a new thought shot across his mind and his lips drew together in a thin, hard line. The road to revenge lay open before him! With an abrupt gesture he stepped forward and pulled back the counterpane.

In the yellow lamp-light the thin face of the dead man had an ashen hue; the half-opened eyes and the prominent teeth, from which the lips had partly receded, confronted him grewsomely. But the force of his disappointment and rage was something before which mere human horror was swept aside. With another rapid movement, he stooped over the bed and unclasped the thin gold chain that hung round the dead man's neck, letting the metal symbol and the long, thin key slip from it into his hand. Turning to the dressing-table, he caught up a lamp; hurried from the room; and, descending the stairs, passed into the study.

To his excited glance the place looked strangely undisturbed. Though the frames of the windows rattled in the gale, the interior arrangements were as precise and bare as usual; the fireless grate stared at him coldly, and against the whitewashed wall the heavy iron safe stood out like an accentuated blot of shadow. Impelled by his one dominating idea, he crossed without an instant's hesitation to the door of this hitherto inviolable repository of his uncle's secrets, and, inserting the key he carried, threw back the massive door.

One glance showed him the thing he sought. Lying in solitary state upon the highest shelf was a heavy book bound in white leather. The edges of the cover were worn yellow with time and use, and from the centre of the binding gleamed the familiar octagonal symbol exquisitely wrought in gold and jewels. With hands that trembled slightly he lifted the book from its place, closed and locked the door of the safe, and, extinguishing the lamp, left the room.

In the flood of unreasoning rage and thwarted hope that surged about him, he had no definite plan regarding the object in his hand. He only knew, by the medium of instinct, that through it he could strike a blow at the uncle who had excluded him from his just inheritance — at the crazy scheme by which he had been defrauded of his due.

With hasty steps he mounted the stairs and re-entered the bedroom. To his agitated mind it seemed but just that, whatever his vengeance, it should be accomplished in the grim, unconscious presence of the dead man.

Stepping into the room, he paused and looked about him, seeking some suggestion. As he stood there, his eyes, by a natural process of inspiration, fell upon the fire that glowed and crackled in the grate; and with a sharp, inarticulate sound of satisfaction he strode forward to the hearth, knelt down, and prepared for his work of destruction.

As he crouched over the flames a fresh gale swept inland from the sea, seizing the house in its fierce embrace; and the red tongues of fire leaped up the chimney in the instant answer of element to element.

Instinctively he bent forward, opened the book and gathered the first sheaf of leaves into his fingers. Then, involuntarily, he paused, as the bold characters of the printed words shot up black and clear in the fierce glow.

Almost without volition he read the opening lines:

"Out of obscurity will He come. And — having proved Himself — no man will question Him. For the Past lies in the Great Unknown. By the Scitsym — from which none but the Chosen may read — will ye know Him; and, knowing Him, ye will bow down — Mystics, Arch-Mystics, and Arch-Councillor alike. And the World will be His. For He will be Power made absolute!"

"For he will be Power made absolute!" Something in the six simple words arrested Henderson, suspended his thoughts and checked his hand. By an odd psychological process his rage became chilled, his mind veered from its point of view. With a curious stiffness of motion he drew away from the fire — the book held uninjured in his hand.

"He will be Power made absolute!" he repeated, mechanically, as he rose slowly to his feet.

CHAPTER III

On a certain night in mid-January, exactly ten years after Andrew Henderson's death, any one of the multitudinous inhabitants of London whom business or pleasure carried to that division of Brompton known as Hellier Crescent, would undoubtedly have been attracted to the house distinguished from its fellows as No. 8.

Outwardly, this house was not remarkable. It possessed the massive portico and the imposing frontage that lend to Hellier Crescent its air of dignified repose; but there its similarity to the surrounding dwellings ended. The basement sent forth no glow of warmth and comfort, as did the neighboring basements; the ground-floor windows permitted no ray of mellow light to slip through the chinks of shutter or curtain. From attic to cellar, the house seemed in darkness, the only suggestion of occupation coming from the occasional drawing back and forth of a small slide that guarded a monastic-looking grating set in the hall door.

And yet towards this unlighted and unfriendly dwelling a thin stream of people — all on foot and all evidently agitated — made their way continuously on that January night between the hours of ten and eleven. The behavior of these people, who differed widely in outward characteristics, was marked by a peculiar fundamental similarity. They all entered the quiet precincts of the Crescent with the same air of subdued excitement; each moved softly and silently towards the darkened house, and, mounting the steps, knocked once upon the heavy door. And each in turn stood patient, while the slide was drawn back, and a voice from within demanded the signal that granted admittance.

This mysterious gathering of forces had continued for nearly an hour when a cab drew up sharply at the corner where Hellier Crescent abuts upon St. George's Terrace, and a lady descended from it. As she handed his fare to the cabman, her face and figure were plainly visible in the light of the street-lamps. The former was pale in coloring, delicately oval in shape, and illumined by a pair of large and unusually brilliant eyes; the latter was tall, graceful, and clad in black.

Having dismissed her cab, the new-comer crossed St.

George's Terrace with an appearance of haste, and entering Hellier Crescent, immediately mounted the steps of No. 8.

The last member of this strange procession had disappeared into the house as she reached the door; but, acting with apparent familiarity, she lifted the knocker and let it fall once.

For a moment there was no response; then, as in the case of the former visitors, the slide was drawn back and a beam of light came through the grating, to be immediately obscured by the shadowy suggestion of a face with two inquiring eyes.

"The Word?" demanded a solemn voice.

The new-comer lifted her head.

"He shall be Power made absolute!" she responded in a low and slightly tremulous voice; and a moment later the door opened, and she stepped into the hall.

The scene inside the house was curious in the extreme. If there were quiet and darkness outside, a brilliant light and a tense, contagious excitement reigned within. The large hall, lighted by tall lamps, was covered with a thick black carpet into which the feet sank noiselessly, and the walls and ceiling were draped in the same sombre tint; but at intervals of a few feet, columns of white marble, chiselled into curious shapes, gleamed upon the observer from shadowy niches.

On ordinary occasions, there was a solemnity, a coldness, in this sombre vestibule; but tonight a strange electric activity seemed to have been breathed upon the atmosphere. Women with flushed faces and men with feverishly bright eyes hurried to and fro in an irrepressible, aimless agitation. A blending of dread and hysterical anticipation was stamped upon every face. People stopped one another with nervous, unstrung gesture and odd, disjointed sentences.

As the last comer entered, she paused for a moment, uncertain and hesitating; but almost as she did so, a remarkable-looking and massively built man who was standing in the hall, disengaged himself from a group of people, and, coming directly towards her, took her hand.

"Mrs. Witcherley! At last!" he exclaimed, in a full, emotional voice. "I looked for you among the gathering and for a moment I almost feared —"

"That I would fail?" Her voice was still tinged with agitation; the pupils of her large eyes were distended.

"No, I did not mean that. But at such a moment we burn lest even one of the Elect be missing." He continued to hold her hand, looking into her face with his prominent dark eyes, from which flashed and glowed an excitement that spread over his whole heavy face.

"The night of nights!" he exclaimed. "To have lived to witness it!" His face glowed with a sudden enthusiasm; and freeing her fingers, he lifted up his right hand. "'He shall walk into your midst — and sit above you as a King!'" he quoted, in a loud voice. Then remembering his companion, he lowered his tone.

"Everything is in readiness," he added, more soberly. "The Precursor still unceasingly prophesies the Advent. Come with me into the Place. The Gathering is all but assembled." Laying his large hand upon her arm, he led her forward unresistingly through the groups of men and women, and onward down a long corridor to where a curtain hid an arched doorway.

For a moment they paused outside this door, and the man — still laboring under some strange excitement — again raised his hand:

"Come!" he cried. "And before we leave the Place, may the Hope of the Universe be fulfilled!" Lifting the curtain, he ushered her through the door.

The room — or chapel — into which they stepped was large and lofty, covered on floor and walls with sections of marble alternately black and white; overhead swung a huge octagonal symbol in jewelled and polished metal; and at the end farthest from the door a haze of incense clouded what appeared to be an altar.

A concourse of people filled every corner of this vast room; and from the crouched or upright figures rose a continuous, inaudible murmuring.

Still guiding his companion, the massively built man forced a way between the closely packed figures. But, half-way up the room, the woman paused and glanced at him.

"This will do," she whispered. "Not any nearer, please. Not

any nearer."

His only answer was to lay his hand upon her arm, and by a persistent pressure to draw her onward up the narrow aisle. Reaching the railed-in space about which the incense hung, he paused in his own turn and motioned her towards the foremost row of seats, from which the majority of the gathering seemed to hold aloof.

With a quick, nervous gesture she deprecated the suggestion. "No! No!" she murmured. "Let me sit behind. Please let me sit behind."

But his fingers tightened impressively upon her arm. "No," he whispered, close to her ear. "No, I want you to be here. When the time arrives, I want the full light to shine upon you."

After this she demurred no more, but moved obediently into the appointed seat, her companion placing himself beside her.

In the first moments of agitation and nervousness, she had scarcely observed her surroundings; but now, as her perturbation partially subsided, she looked back at the rows of bowed or erect figures, and forward at the space about which the incense clung like a filmy veil. At a first glance this veil seemed almost too dense to penetrate; but as her sight grew accustomed to its drifting whiteness, she was able to discern the objects that lay behind.

In place of the altar, usually prominent in every religious building, there was a wide semicircular space, within which stood a gold chair raised upon a dais and a heavy lectern of symbolic design on which rested a white leather book, worn yellow at the edges. Over this book a man was poring, apparently unconscious of the active interest he evoked. He was short and thick-set, with a square jaw, a long upper lip, and keen eyes. Over a head of vividly red hair, he wore a round black silk cap, and his figure was enveloped in a flowing black gown.

From time to time, as he read, he lifted one hand in rapt excitement, while his lips moved unceasingly in rapid, inaudible speech. At last, with a sudden dramatic gesture, he turned from the lectern and threw out both arms towards the high gold chair.

"Oh, empty throne! Empty world!" he cried. "Be filled!"

There was something intense, something electric in the

words. A startled cry broke from the people, already wrought to nervous tension. Some among them rose to their feet; some glanced fearfully behind them; others cowered upon the ground.

And then — in what precise manner no one present ever remembered — the curtain at the doorway of the chapel was swung sharply back; and the tall, straight figure of a man clad all in white moved slowly up the aisle.

He moved forward calmly and deliberately, his gaze fixed, his senses apparently unconscious of the many eyes and tongues from which frightened glances and frightened, awe-struck words escaped as he made his solitary, impressive progress.

Reaching the railing, he paused and lifted one hand as if in benediction towards the red-haired man who still remained in solitary occupation of the Sanctuary.

At the action, a gasp went up from the crowded chapel, and even those who still crouched upon the floor ventured to raise their heads and glance at the spot where the tall figure in the white serge robe stood motionless and impressive. Then the whole concourse of devotees stirred in involuntary excitement as the red-haired man, with a cry of rapture, rushed forward and prostrated himself at the feet of the stranger.

For a space, that to the watchers seemed interminable, the two central figures remained rigid; then at last the tall man stooped, and with great dignity raised the other.

As he gained his feet, it was obvious that the smaller man was deeply agitated. His lips were trembling with some strange emotion, and it seemed that he could scarcely command his gestures. After a protracted moment of struggle, however, he appeared to regain his self-control; for with a slightly tremulous movement he stepped forward, laid his hands on the low railing and glanced at the assembled people.

"Mystics!" he began. "Chosen Ones! Out of the Unseen I have come to prophesy to you — I, an obscure servant and follower of the Mighty. For fifteen days have I spoken — telling you that which was at hand. And now, behold I am justified!" He paused and indicated the tall white figure still standing motionless, with face averted from the congregation.

"What have I told you!" he continued, his voice rising. "Have I not quoted from the sacred Scitsym — which until this hour I have never been permitted to look upon? Have I not foretold the coming of this man — the garments he would wear — the Sign upon his person? And have I not done these things by a power outside myself?" Again his voice rose; and the congregation thrilled in response.

"You have listened to me — you have marvelled — but in your Souls doubt has held sway. Now is the moment of justification! It is not meet that the Great One should plead for recognition; it is for you — the Watchers — to see and claim him. Master!" he cried, suddenly. "Master, show them the Sign!"

A hush like the hush of night fell upon the people; and in this curious and impressive lull the white-robed man turned slowly round facing the congregation.

His appearance was arresting and remarkable, though it possessed nothing of beauty. He had a tall and powerful figure, a strong and determined face; his bare head was covered with close-cut black hair; his hard, firm lips were clean-shaven, and his gray eyes looked across the chapel with a peculiar sombre fire.

He stood silent for a moment, surveying the faces clustered before him; then he raised his left hand.

"My People!" he began, in a deep, slow voice. "We live in an age when doubt roams through the world like a beast of prey. I ask not for the faith that accepts blindly; but in this most sacred Scitsym —" he pointed to the white book upon the lectern — "it is written that, by a certain secret Sign, the Arch-Mystics will recognize Him for whom they have waited. I call upon the Arch-Mystics to declare whether or no I bear upon my person that secret Sign!" He paused for a moment; then with a grave, calm gesture he unfastened his robe where it crossed his breast and threw it open.

There was a rustle of intense curiosity, as all involuntarily leaned forward; an audible gasp of awe and shrinking, as all instinctively drew back before the sight that confronted them. Across the Prophet's breast, in marks of a cruel laceration, ran the symbolic octagonal figure of the Mystic sect.

He stood dignified and unmoved until the tremor of emotion

had subsided. Then his glance travelled over the foremost row of seats.

"Come forth!" he commanded, authoritatively. "Come forth and acknowledge me!" His eyes moved slowly from seat to seat — pausing momentarily on the pale, absorbed face of the woman in black. But scarcely had his glance rested upon her than the heavily built man who sat beside her, rose agitatedly and stepped forward to the sanctuary. For a space he stood staring at the scarred skin from which the symbol of his creed stood forth as if miraculously branded; then he turned to the congregation, his prominent eyes burning, his heavy face working with emotion.

"Brethren," he said, inarticulately. "Brethren, it is indeed the Sign!"

But the Prophet remained motionless.

"Where are the other five?" he asked, in a level voice.

Almost simultaneously four men rose from the congregation and came forward. One was tall and gaunt, with a Slavonic type of face, wild eyes, and a long, fair beard; another was young — scarcely more than seven and twenty — with the free carriage, fiery glance, and swarthy complexion of the nomadic races of southeastern Europe; the third was a small, frail man of fifty, with a nervous system painfully in advance of his physical strength; while the fourth was a true mystic — impassioned, enthusiastic, detached. One by one these men advanced, examined the scars, and turning to the people, confirmed the words of their fellow. Then, amid a tremulous hush, the last of the six — the Arch-Councillor himself — was led up the aisle.

For an instant the glimmering of some new feeling crossed the Prophet's face, as his glance rested on the old man who slowly approached with feeble steps, bent back, and anxious, sightless eyes. But, as quickly as it had come, the expression passed, and he stepped forward for the old man's touch.

With a quivering gesture the Arch-Councillor lifted his hand and nervously passed his fingers over the scars; then, drawing the Prophet down, he touched his face. For a long moment of suspense his fingers lingered over the features; then they fell again upon the scars. And an instant later he sank upon his knees.

"It is indeed made manifest!" he cried, in a loud, unsteady voice. "He shall sit above you as upon a Throne!"

The words were magical. The whole concourse of people swayed forward hysterically. Men pressed upward towards the railing; women wept.

And through it all the Prophet stood unmoved. He stood like a rock against which the clamorous human sea beat wildly. With a quiet movement he drew his robe across his breast, hiding the unsightly scars, but otherwise he made no motion. At last the red-haired man who had first claimed him, stepped forward to his side.

"Speak to them, Master!" he said.

The words roused the Prophet. With a calm gesture he raised his head, his eyes confronting the mass of strained, excited faces lifted to his.

"My People," he said again, in his deep voice. "What will you do with me?"

The response was instant.

"The Throne! The Throne!" The crowd surged forward in a wave, then receded as the tide recedes; and the old Arch-Councillor stepped feebly into the Sanctuary and extended his hands to the Prophet.

It was a moment of breathless awe. The tall woman, who until that moment had remained seated, involuntarily rose to her feet.

She saw the figure of the Prophet move grandly across the Sanctuary in the wake of the old blind man; she saw him halt for an infinitesimal space at the foot of the throne; she saw him calmly and decisively mount the steps of the dais and seat himself in the golden chair. Then, prompted by an overwhelming impulse, she yielded to the spirit of the moment and dropped to her knees.

CHAPTER IV

Three hours later, when the curious rite of acknowledgment had been completed and the concourse of zealots had departed from Hellier Crescent, the first night in his new kingdom opened for the Prophet. As the clocks of Brompton were striking two, the six Arch-Mystics — each of whom possessed rooms in a remote portion of the house — lingeringly and fearfully bade him goodnight, and left him alone with the Precursor in the apartments that for nearly fifty years had been kept swept and garnished in expectation of his advent.

Apart from their suggestion of the mystical and fantastic, these rooms possessed an intrinsic interest of their own. And some consciousness of this interest appeared to be at work within the Prophet's mind; for scarcely had he and his companion been assured of privacy, than he rose from the massive ivory chair which had been apportioned to him and from which he had made his second and private justification of his claims; and very slowly and deliberately began a circuit of the chamber.

With engrossed attention he passed from one to another of the rare and costly objects that formed the furniture of the place; while, from the ebony table in the centre of the room, his red-haired companion watched him with vigilant eyes.

Still moving with unruffled deliberation, he completed his tour of the apartment; then a remarkable — a startling thing took place. He wheeled round, laid his hands heavily on the Precursor's shoulders, and looking closely into his face, broke into speech.

"Well?" he demanded, intensely. "Well? Well? What have you to say?"

At first the red-haired man sat watching him, mute and motionless; then with a suddenness equal to his own, he released himself, leaned forward in his chair, and silently uncorked a gold flask that stood upon the table before him. Lifting it high, he poured some wine into two glass goblets, and without a word handed one to the white-robed Prophet, and himself picked up the other.

"John," he said, deliberately, "you were magnificent! Let me give you a toast? Power! Power made Absolute!"

With a grave gesture the Prophet extended his hand, and their glasses clinked.

"Power made Absolute!" he responded, in a low, deep voice.

In silence they drank the toast; but, as he replaced his glass upon the table, the Prophet shook off his gravity, and turned again to his companion.

"Now!" he exclaimed. "Now! Out with it all! How much of this has been native adroitness, and how much unbelievable good-fortune? Out with it! I'm hungry and thirsty for the truth."

For answer the Precursor slowly lifted the gold flask and replenished his own glass. "Truth in a golden flask! But, to throw a sop to your curiosity, it was a matter of native genius engineered by Providence. I don't mind admitting that when I stood on the doorstep of this house fifteen nights ago and knocked the mystic knock, I felt like a man embarking on a coffin-ship." He stopped to drain his glass.

The Prophet took a step forward.

"And then?" he said, eagerly. "Then?"

The other waved his empty glass.

"Oh, there entered the native genius of Terence Dominick Devereaux! Under that tremendous escort I stormed the citadel —"

The Prophet smiled. "And the Mystic ears, I have no doubt."

For a third time the Precursor filled his glass.

"The tongue is mightier — and a good deal more portable — than either the pen or the sword, John," he said, sagely. "Paving your way with words has been an unrecognized work of art. But how about yourself? I have my own curiosity." He wheeled round in his seat and looked into his companion's face.

The Prophet looked away.

"Oh, I had my qualms, too!" he said, slowly. "Just for a moment the world seemed to tremble, when the old Arch-Councillor groped forward and put his hands over my face. It swept me off my feet — swept me back ten years. It was like a vision in a crystal — if such a thing could exist. I saw the whole past scene.

The bare room — the old dead man — myself; the overwhelming wish to avenge my wrongs, and the sudden suggestion that turned the wish cold. I saw the long, bleak night in which I completed the colossal task of copying the Scitsym line for line; I saw the gray morning steal in across the room as I closed the book, returned it to its safe and replaced the key on my uncle's neck in preparation for the arrival of the Arch-Councillor. It all passed before my mind, and then in a flash was gone. I ceased to be John Henderson."

The Precursor glanced quickly towards the door.

"Avoid that name. Habits grow — and so do suspicions. Your probation has been too long and too hard to permit us to run risks. Now that you've stepped into your kingdom —" He made an expressive gesture.

The Prophet laughed shortly, then suddenly turned grave again.

"You are right!" he said. "Only a man with a light conscience can skate on thin ice. To return to our original subject, what about the inner workings of this odd game? It is so curious to have lived for years on theory, and suddenly to come face to face with practice. I tell you I'm starving for facts." He stepped forward quickly and dropped into a chair that faced his companion's.

"Out with it all! To begin, who is the master-spirit? You know what I mean. The master-spirit in the true sense. Poor old blind Arian doesn't stand for much."

The Precursor looked meditatively at his empty glass.

"No," he said, thoughtfully. "You touch truth there! Michael Arian is the cipher; Bale-Corphew's the meaning. Bale-Corphew is an interesting man, John — I had almost said a dangerous man —"

The Prophet's lip curled slightly.

"Dangerous!"

"Yes; dangerous in a sense. In the sense that a personality always is dangerous. Among the six Arch-Mystics there is, to my thinking, only one *man*, and he interests me. He interests me, does Horatio Bale-Corphew!"

The Prophet leaned forward in his chair.

"I think I catch your meaning," he said. "Something of the same idea occurred to me when he rose from his seat tonight. While we spied upon them in the last six months, he always struck me as curiously un-English, with that sleek exterior and those flashing eyes of his. But in the chapel tonight he was almost aggressively alien. When he touched my arm I could literally feel him bristle."

The other nodded.

"You've said it!" he cried. "Horatio bristles! His whole queer soul is in this business — every fibre of it. He attempts no division of allegiance — except, perhaps, in the matter of the heart —"

The Prophet glanced up and smiled.

"The heart? Do my faithful Watchers permit themselves hearts? The Scitsym makes no provision for such frail organs."

The Precursor laughed again.

"Oh, we Elect are by no means free from little saving weaknesses! That's where we become dramatic. You can't have effect without contrast. Horatio, for instance, is instinctively dramatic."

"Indeed!"

"Yes. Oh yes! I know what I'm saying. I've studied them all. More than once, when my Soul has been communing with your August Spirit, I have watched Horatio's dramatic contrast from the corner of my eyes."

Again the Prophet smiled.

"The contrast frequents the chapel then?"

"Frequents? Undoubtedly. Horatio has literally swept her into the fold. She was here tonight to bend the knee to you."

A look of recollection crossed the Prophet's eyes.

"Tonight?" he said. "Not the woman who sat beside him? The woman with the big eyes? She and Bale-Corphew! The idea is absurd!"

"Undeniable, nevertheless. I have deduced the story. The lady is a widow — no relations — too much freedom — vague aspirations after the ideal. She has sounded society and found it too shallow; sounded philosophy and found it too deep; and upon her horizon of desires and disappointments has loomed the colossal presence of Bale-Corphew — enthusiast, mystic, leader of a fascinatingly unorthodox sect. What is the result? The lady — too feminine to be truly modern, too modern to be wholly womanly — is viewing life through new glasses, and by their medium seeing Horatio invested with a halo otherwise invisible."

The Prophet remained quiet and silent; then he rose slowly from his seat and walked round the table. "Devereaux," he said, laconically, "only the Prophet is going to wear a halo here."

The Precursor's sharply marked, expressive eyebrows went up in quick comment.

"Can even a latter-day Prophet afford autocracy?"

For a space the Prophet made no response; then he took a step forward and laid his hand impressively on his friend's shoulder.

"Devereaux," he said, in a new voice — a voice that unconsciously held something of the command that had marked it in the chapel — "the Prophet of the Mystics has come to rule. He has not come to follow the laws that others — that men like Bale-Corphew — have seen fit to make. He has come to be a law unto himself!"

CHAPTER V

It is astonishing in how short a space of time a man of vigorous character can make his personality felt. On the night of his mysterious advent, the Prophet had found his people in a condition of mental chaos — as liable to repudiate as to accept the seeker for their confidence; but before one month had passed he had, by domination of will, so moulded this neurotic mass of humanity that his own position had gradually and insensibly merged from suppliant into that of autocrat. Without a murmur of doubt or dissension the Mystics had proclaimed him their king.

On the last day of the thirty he sat alone in his room — the room in which he and the red-haired Precursor had held their private council on the night of his coming. The heavy purple curtains that shielded the windows were partly drawn, throwing a subdued, almost a devotional, light over the wide, imposing apartment and across the ebony table, on which rested the sacred Scitsym, surrounded by an array of smaller and more ancient books, several rolls of parchment, a number of quill pens, and a dish of ink. It was at this table that the Prophet sat; he wore the monastic white robe that he always affected in presence of his people, his arms were folded, and his face looked calm and grave, as though he appreciated the moment's solitude.

The solitude, however, was not destined to endure. The soft booming of a gong presently roused him to attention, and a moment later the door of the apartment opened and an ascetic-looking man, whose duty and privilege it was to wait upon him, entered deferentially.

He stood for a moment in an attitude of profound abasement; then he stepped forward and stood beside the table.

"Master," he said, in a low voice. "The newest among us would speak with you!"

The Prophet raised his head and a gleam of interest crossed his eyes; but almost immediately he subdued the look.

"I am willing," he replied, unemotionally, in the usual formula. Then he glanced at his attendant. "After this, the audiences for the day are over," he added.

The man bowed, and with awe-struck deference moved silently from the room, almost immediately reappearing, to usher in the devotee, and with the same conscious air of mystery, to retire, closing the heavy door.

For a moment the new-comer stood just inside the threshold. As on the night of the Prophet's coming, she wore a long, black dress that accentuated her height and grace, and brought into prominence the clear pallor of her skin and the remarkable luminous brilliance of her eyes. A struggle between superstitious dread and human curiosity was distinctly visible in her expression as she stood uncertain of her position, doubtful as to her first move.

The Prophet glanced at her, and the shadow of a smile touched his lips.

"Have no fear," he said. "Come forward!"

The strong, steady voice gave her courage, and with slightly agitated haste she stepped towards the table.

The Prophet gravely motioned her to a seat and assumed an attitude of attention. Upon each of the thirty mornings he had sat in this same position in his ivory chair, while, one after another, the members of the sect had claimed audience with him. Morning after morning he had exhibited the same grave, aloof interest — his hands clasped, his eyes upon the Scitsym — while the fearful, the fanatical, the hysterical had poured forth their tales of struggle or aspiration. But now, on this last morning, he was conscious of a new suggestion, a new impression in what had grown to be routine. This last aspirant for spiritual light was neither fanatical nor hysterical, was scarcely even imbued with fear. Something within his brain responded to the idea, to the reassuring human curiosity that gleamed in her eyes. He found himself waiting for her first words with an impatience that no other member of the congregation had aroused.

But the wait was long — disconcertingly long. The aspirant glanced uncertainly about the room, as if unwilling or unable to break into speech; then at last she raised her head, and, with an effort, met the Prophet's eyes.

"I'm terribly nervous!" she said, in an irresistibly feminine voice.

The effect upon her hearer was instantaneous. The distant and spiritual aloofness, so easy to assume in the presence of the credulous, became suddenly a matter of impossibility. With a quiet dignity that had more of masculine protectiveness than of mystical inspiration he turned to her afresh.

"Have no fear!" he answered, gently. "My only desire is to help you. Tell me everything that is in your mind."

She leaned forward quickly. "You — you are most kind —" she began. Then again she halted.

But he took no notice of her embarrassment.

"Why have you never come before?" he asked. "Had you no doubts to be set at rest?" He spoke so quietly that her nervousness forsook her, and with a swift impulse she glanced up at him.

"I — I think I was afraid," she said, candidly. "You see, I am not exactly one of the others —"

"You did not quite believe that the One you had waited for had really come?" His voice was low and tinged with some inscrutable meaning.

"Oh no! No; it was not that. Before you came, I confess I was sceptical; I confess I did not believe that any one would come, that there was any truth — any real meaning — in the sect. But then — when you did come —"

The Prophet lifted his head.

"When I did come?" he asked, sharply.

"The whole thing was different —"

"The whole thing was different?" he repeated, slowly and meditatively. By a curious process of suggestion and recollection, something of his own experiences in the realm of mental upheaval rose with her words. He studied the pale face and brilliant eresh and more intimate interest.

"The whole thing was different?" he said once more, in his slow, deep voice.

The warm color flooded her face. "Yes," she admitted. "Yes. You seemed the one real person — the one sane thing in the whole ceremony. I felt — I knew that you were — strong." She paused, alarmed at her own timidity; and again their eyes met.

"And why have you never come to me before?" He had no

particular meaning in the question; he was only conscious of an inexplicable wish to prolong the interview.

"Oh, I don't know — I scarcely know." Again she spoke quickly and nervously. "I have come every night to hear you speak — I have loved to hear you speak. But — but to be alone with you —" She paused, expressively. "It is all so strange — so extraordinary. It doesn't seem to belong to the present day —" She looked up at him in appealing perplexity.

"And why did you come now?"

"Why? Oh, because — because I could not stay away."

For the first time the Prophet was conscious of a tremor of discomfiture; for the first time the spectacle of his fraud, as seen from a point of view other than his own, touched him unpleasantly. He moved slightly in his massive chair.

"In this life," he said, with a sudden, almost incontinent assumption of his Prophetic manner, "we must be ever careful to distinguish the Wine from the Vessel that contains it. I endeavor, with all the Power I am possessed of, to impress upon my People that I have come, not to *be* the Way, but to *show* the Way! To teach you all that what you seek in me, is in each one of you. Every man is his own Prophet, if he but knew it!" As he spoke he turned his eyes upon the Scitsym, and the hard, inscrutable look that so dominated his followers descended upon his face. As he reached the last words, he glanced again at his companion, but as his eyes rested on her face he paused disconcerted. She was gazing at him with a candid, spontaneous admiration infinitely more human and infinitely more irresistible than the neurotic adoration that was daily lavished on him. With an odd, inexplicable sense of guilt, he rose quickly from his seat.

"Do not forget — do not allow yourself to forget that this is my teaching," he said. "That you have each within yourselves the thing you demand in me. Look for it within yourselves! Rely upon yourselves!"

As he ceased, she also rose. She was pale, and trembled slightly.

"But if one cannot follow that teaching?" she asked. "If one longs to rely upon some one else? If one cannot rely upon one's self?"

The Prophet made no answer. He stood with one hand resting on the table, his gaze fixed upon the book.

Emboldened by his silence, she approached him by a step.

"I think I could believe —" she murmured. "I think I could believe — anything, if I might learn it from you." She paused pleadingly; then, as he still stood unresponsive, the color rushed again into her face.

"I — I have been presumptuous," she said. "I have offended you."

Something in her tone, in her charming unaffected humility stung him. For the first time in his career as Prophet, the blood surged hotly and painfully into his face.

"Do not say that!" he began, impulsively; then he checked himself. "I am here to teach my People," he added. "All my People — without exception."

For one moment she studied his face half doubtfully; then at last her own emotions conquered her doubt.

"Then I may come again?"

He did not reply at once; and when at last his words did come, his voice was unusually irresolute and low.

"You may come — at any time," he said, without meeting her eyes.

CHAPTER VI

So it came about that the serpent of misgiving entered into the Prophet's paradise. With Enid Witcherley's words, the realization of his true position had been unpleasantly suggested to him, and the grain of doubt had been scattered over the banquet he had set himself to enjoy. It was one thing to fool men who yearned to be fooled — even to fool women whose peculiarities set them apart from their sex; but it was indisputably another matter to dupe a young and confiding girl, who came with all the fascination of modern doubt, counterbalanced by the charm of feminine credulity.

Long after she left him, he had paced up and down the room in perplexity of spirit, until at last, with a sudden contempt for his own weakness, he had turned to where the white binding of the Scitsym caught the subdued light. The sight of the book had nerved him, as it never failed to do; but for all his regained firmness, the sense of uneasy shame had remained with him during the day; and that night, when he addressed his people, he had instinctively guarded his glance from resting on the seats that fronted the Sanctuary.

But now that first interview was past by three weeks, and Enid's daily visits to the great room where he gave audience to the congregation had become one of the recognized events of the twenty-four hours. The sense of shame returned periodically; but on each renewal of the feeling he salved his conscience more and more successfully with the assurance that to her, as to himself, the Mystics were in reality nothing but the products of a neurotic age — mere hysterical dabblers in the truths of the universe. She was too delicately feminine, he told himself with growing conviction, too intelligent and self-controlled, to be more than temporarily attracted to any such exotic creed. She might toy with it for a while, but the day must inevitably dawn when common-sense and the need of surer things would send her back into the broad channel of simple, satisfying Christianity. For a space this unnatural state of things would last; for a space their curious companionship would continue — their long, intimate talks would make life something new and wonderful; then — But there, for some unexplained reason, speculation invariably stopped.

So things stood on the fiftieth morning after her first coming. The stream of suppliants for his favor was all but exhausted, and he awaited to give the last audience of the day.

After the moment of quiet and solitude that always separated the interviews, the sonorous gong announced the last visitor; the silent, ascetic attendant threw open the door and Enid entered.

This time she displayed none of the hesitancy that had marked her early manner. She came towards the table with quick, assured steps, her face bright with anticipation.

As she approached, the Prophet rose. It was remarkable that he no longer retained his sitting position when she entered the room, as was his custom with the other members of the sect. Involuntarily and almost unconsciously he extended to her the ordinary courtesies that man instinctively offers to woman.

As she reached the table, she glanced up at him, and something of the pleasure died out of her face.

"You look tired," she said, softly.

He smiled.

"Does that disappoint you?"

His tone confused her.

"Oh no! No!" Then she colored slightly and glanced at him again. "Why do you ask?"

"Because it is the way of humanity to refuse any common weakness to its leaders — spiritual or temporal."

Again a wave of color crossed her skin. "But surely —"

"Surely what?"

She glanced away; then, seeming to gather up her courage, she looked back at him.

"I mean," she said, slowly, "that some people are so strong that they may be allowed to have anything —"

"Even weaknesses —" Once more he smiled. It was significant how, gradually and indisputably, the tone of teacher had dropped out of his conversation. Neither could have told the date on which the change had occurred — perhaps neither was conscious that it had even taken place. But the fact remained that, with her, he no longer felt compelled to hold aloof; that, with her, he had discarded the allegorical manner of speech, and had begun to show himself as he naturally was.

"Even weaknesses?" he said again, as she made no attempt to answer.

At the words her eyes once more met his.

"Yes," she said, with new resolution — "yes, even weaknesses. I often think that it is because you are so — so human that you hold us as you do. It seems right that a Prophet should belong to the people he has come to teach. All the prophets of the world have essentially belonged to their own times. If you had sat upon the Throne all day and communed with your Soul, I should have been very much afraid of you; but I should never have believed in you as I do now, when you talk to me and advise me and help me like — like a friend." Her voice trembled slightly.

A peculiar expression crossed the Prophet's face.

"So I seem a — friend?"

"More than a friend. I can never tell you what you have been to me — what you have done for me. I have never been so happy — so satisfied in my life, as in these last three weeks. Every disappointment and dissatisfaction seems to have slipped away; I seem to have been living in some calm, beautiful, restful atmosphere —" She paused, her face as well as her voice tinged with a subtle excitement.

"It may be very selfish, but I wish that these days could go on forever. I know that, for you, they are only a probation; that you must crave for the moment when, having taught us everything, you will go out into the world and teach the Unbelievers. I know all that, and I know it is only right, but — but I hate to think of it!" A sudden break came in her voice.

"You hate to think that all this must end?"

Again their eyes met; but, as though the contact of glances embarrassed her, Enid looked away.

"Yes, I do hate it. Do you despise me for being so selfish — so jealous of those other people who will take our place?"

For a moment the Prophet made no reply. In the dim light of the room, the muscles of his hard face looked set; his strong hands were clasped.

"Do you despise me?" she asked again.

"It is not for me to judge any one — you least of all," he answered, without looking at her.

At the subdued tone, the unexpected words, she turned to him apprehensively.

"You are angry with me?"

"Indeed, no."

"Then what is it? What have I done — or said?"

He remained silent.

In her sudden distress she leaned forward in her chair, looking into his face with new solicitude.

"I know — I feel that I have displeased you. Won't you tell me what I have done?"

As she put the question, she laid one gloved hand upon the table; and though the Prophet's eyes were fixed upon the Scitsym, he was conscious in every fibre of the appeal the unstudied gesture made — as he was poignantly conscious of the clear eyes, the soft dark hair, the questioning upturned face.

For an interminable time the silence remained unbroken; at last, with a little sound of fresh distress, Enid bent still nearer.

"Oh, I understand!" she exclaimed. "I understand! You think I have taken advantage of your goodness. You think I have imagined that, because you are kind and patient and tolerant, I might look upon you as — as a man." As she said the word she paused, frightened by her own timidity.

But as suddenly the Prophet wheeled round and laid his fingers over hers. The pressure of his hand was like steel, the expression of his face was altered and disturbed.

"If you only knew —" he said, sharply — "if you only knew how I have longed to hear you say just that one word *man!*" He paused almost triumphantly, his eyes searching her frightened face, his fingers gripping hers.

For an instant she sat petrified and fascinated; then a faint sound of alarm escaped her, and she turned towards the door.

Without the formality of the announcing gong, two men had entered the room, and stood silent spectators of the tableau. One was Devereaux, the Precursor; the other was Horatio Bale-Corphew.

For one embarrassed moment all four looked at each other; then the Precursor hastened to save the situation. He made a long, profound obeisance, and stepped deferentially to the table.

"Your pardon, Master!" he murmured. "We knew not that the immutable Soul was speaking from within you, calling one among us towards the Light!" He glanced quickly over his shoulder to where the massive form and agitated face of Bale-Corphew was framed in the doorway.

At his peremptory look the Arch-Mystic seemed to gather himself together. Stepping forward, he made a slightly tardy reverence.

"Master," he said, huskily, "what the Precursor tells you is the truth. Seeing the threshold unguarded, we concluded that the audiences for the day were over." His prominent brown eyes were filled with conflicting expressions as he turned them on the Prophet.

But the Prophet remained unmoved. The hard look had returned to his face, the stern rigidity to his figure. Very slowly he released the hand that still trembled under his own.

"The time of the Prophet belongs to his People," he said, with dignity. "He holds audience whenever, wherever, and *however* it is expedient. Speak, my son! In what can I serve you?"

Bale-Corphew looked at him in silence. Whatever he had come to say appeared to have escaped his mind. For a while inaction reigned in the room; then, with a pale face and nervous manner, Enid rose, bowed to the Prophet, and moved noiselessly to the door.

All three watched her until she had disappeared; then Bale-Corphew found voice again.

"Master," he murmured, hurriedly, "with your permission, I also would leave the Presence;" and with a perturbed gesture, he too bowed and passed out of the room.

CHAPTER VII

On a crisp, cold afternoon, one week after her interview with the Prophet, Enid Witcherley sat in the drawing-room of her London flat. The early portion of the day had been pleasantly warmed and brightened by the pale March sunshine; but at three o'clock a searching wind had begun to blow across the city from the east; and now, as the small gold clock on her bureau chimed the hour of five, she rose from the couch where she had been sitting, and, crossing the room with a little shiver, drew a chair to the fire and pressed the electric bell.

As the maid appeared, in answer to her summons, she gave her order without looking round.

"Tea, Norris!" she said, in an unusually curt and laconic voice.

For a considerable time after the maid's departure she sat motionless, her hands stretched out towards the blazing logs, her large eyes absently watching the fire-light on her many and beautiful rings. When the woman reappeared, and, noiselessly arranging the tea-table, moved it to her side, she scarcely glanced up; and to the most superficial observer it would have been patent that her own thoughts and speculations fully absorbed her mind.

She retained her contemplative attitude after the servant had withdrawn for the second time, and it is doubtful how long she would have remained sunk in apparent lethargy had not the unexpected sound of the hall-door bell caused her to start into an upright position with a little exclamation of surprise and impatience.

As she sat listening with nervous intentness, the door opened, and once more Norris appeared. After a second's hesitation she crossed to her mistress.

"There's a gentleman at the door, ma'am," she said, deprecatingly.

Enid looked up, a frown still darkening her forehead.

"I told you I was not at home."

"I know, ma'am, but —" Norris hesitated.

"But what? I told you I was not to be disturbed. I *won't* be disturbed." With a gesture plainly indicative of high-strung nerves, she turned to the table and poured herself out a cup of tea.

The maid glanced behind her towards the door. "But the gentleman won't go, ma'am —"

"Won't go!" In her surprise Enid laid down the cup she had been about to raise to her lips. "Who is he?" she demanded.

Norris looked down. "I don't know, ma'am. I told him you were not at home, but he won't go. He's the sort of gentleman who won't take no for an answer."

"I don't understand you. Who is he? What is he like?" Unconsciously and involuntarily Enid's tone quickened. Something in the woman's words — something undefined and yet suggestive — stirred and agitated her.

Norris seemed to choose her words. "Well, ma'am," she answered, slowly, "he's very tall — and not like any other gentleman that comes here. I can't rightly explain it, miss, he seems used to having his own way —"

As she halted, uncertain how to choose her words, Enid rose nervously. She could not have defined her emotions, but some feeling at once vague and portentous was working in her mind.

"Did he give no name?"

"No, ma'am. I was to say that he was some one that must be seen. He'd give no name."

For a further instant Enid was silent, conscious of nothing but her own unsteady pulses; then suddenly she turned almost angrily upon the servant.

"Show him in!" she cried. "Show him in at once! Don't keep him standing at the door."

In some confusion Norris turned and walked across the room. At the doorway she paused and looked back.

"Will you have the lights on, ma'am?"

"No. No; the fire makes light enough. I like twilight and a fire. Don't stand waiting!"

The woman departed; and for a space that seemed to her interminable, Enid stood beside the fireplace, motionless with hope, dread, and an almost uncontrollable nervousness. At last, as in a dream, she saw the door open and the tall, characteristic figure of the Prophet move into the room.

She was vaguely aware that he halted for a moment, as if undecided as to his action, while Norris retired, softly closing the door. Then, with a sudden leap of the heart, she was conscious that he was coming towards her across the shadowed room.

He moved straight forward until he was close beside her; and, with one of his decisive, imperious gestures, he put out both hands and caught hers.

"It was a case of Mohammed and the mountain!" he said, in his grave voice. "You wouldn't come to me; I *had* to come to you."

No sound escaped her. She stood before him mutely, her face paling and flushing, her hands fluttering in his.

There was a slight pause; and again he bent towards her.

"Why have you stayed away?"

She hesitated for a moment, spellbound by her emotion; then, making a sudden effort, she looked up. "I — I was afraid." Her voice was so low and shaken that the words were a mere whisper.

"Afraid? Afraid of what?"

She made no answer.

"Of what? Of Bale-Corphew?" He gave a slight, sarcastic laugh.

"No!" She looked up sharply. "Oh no!"

"Then of what? Of me?" His voice suddenly sank, and the pressure of his fingers tightened.

"No! Oh, I don't know! I don't know!" With a tremulous gesture she tried to withdraw her hands.

At the movement, he suddenly drew her towards him. "Tell me!" he said. "I want to know. I must know!"

For the first time since he had entered the room, her glance rested fully on his face. The light was uncertain, but as her gaze concentrated itself, a new look — a look of wonder and alarm — sprang across her eyes. In the seven days since they had spoken together, a change had fallen on him. Some alteration she could not define had grown into his expression; the cold mastery of himself and others was still visible; but a new emotion had insensibly been created — something powerful and even dominant — for which she could find no name. With a sharp, instinctive alarm, her lips parted.

"What is it?" she said, apprehensively. "Why are you here? The time has not come for you to go out into the world?"

A faintly ironic smile flitted across his lips.

"Surely, if one is a Prophet, one can alter even prophecies."

He said the words deliberately, looking down into her face.

The tone, the intentional flippancy of the words, came to her with a shock. It was as if, by considered action, he had set about jeopardizing his own dignity. A chill of undefined apprehension blew across her mind like a cold wind.

"I — I don't understand," she stammered. "How did you get here? How did you get away?"

Again his keen eyes searched hers.

"As for getting away," he said, slowly, "when a Prophet has a Precursor, he should be able to arrange these things. Five o'clock is a dull hour at Hellier Crescent. The Arch-Mystics are perusing the Scitsym; the Precursor is guarding the sacred threshold of the Prophet; the Prophet is — presumably — communing with his Soul. The routine of this evening differs in no way from the routine of any other evening — except that the Precursor is rather more than usually vigilant in his watch." Again the forced flippancy was apparent; and to Enid, staring at him with wide, perplexed eyes, there was something inexplicable and alarming in this new and unfamiliar attitude. With a tremor of foreboding, her glance travelled over his face.

"Has anything happened?" she asked. "Have the People done wrong? Have you — have you been called elsewhere?" At the last dread possibility her voice faltered.

But the Prophet stood cold and almost rigid. At last, by an immense effort, he seemed to gather himself together for some tremendous end.

"Enid," he said, gravely, "I don't know how much you know of life, but I presume you know very little. I presume that — and shall act on the presumption. I shall not expect — even ask — any leniency of you.

"I came here this evening to tell you something that will alter your opinion of me so effectually that nothing hereafter can reinstate me in your mind." He spoke slowly and deliberately, without tremor or falter. Whatever of struggle lay behind his words, it lay with the past. It was evident as he stood there in the pretty, luxurious room, that he possessed a purpose, and that he held to it without thought of a retrograde step.

"I have come to make a confession," he said, quietly. "Not because I believe in the habit of unburdening one's conscience, but because there is something you have a right to know —"

"I — ? A right to know?" Her lips paled.

"Yes. A right to know." With a sudden access of feeling he dropped her hands and turned towards the window, where the last glimmer of the wintry twilight showed through the soft silk curtains.

"I am putting myself in your hands," he said, steadily. "I am jeopardizing myself utterly by what I am going to say; but it seems to me the only way by which I can make — well, can patch up some poor amends —

"I may be presumptuous, but I believe — I think — that I have stood for something in your eyes." He turned and looked at her. But in the mingled dusk and firelight only the pale outline of her face was visible.

"Enid!" he cried, with sudden resolution, "it must be faced. It must be said. I'm not what you think me. I'm a fraud — a lie — an impostor. No more a Prophet — no more inspired than you — or Bale-Corphew!" He stopped abruptly and drew a slow, deep breath.

The pause that followed was long and strained. In the grip of strong emotions, each stood rigid, striving vainly to read the other's face. At last, goaded by the silence, he spoke again.

"You have done this!" he cried. "You have compelled me to tell you! I came to these people; I duped them — and gloried in duping them. I despised them, understood them, traded on them without a scruple. Then you came. You came — and the scheme was shattered. The whole thing, that had bubbled and sparkled, became suddenly like flat champagne. That is a common simile, but it is descriptive. The acting of an actor depends upon his audience. While my audience was composed of fools, I fooled them;

but when you came — you with your scepticism, your curiosity, your feminine dependency — I lost my cue. I became conscious of the footlights and the make-up." Again he paused; and again he endeavored to read her face. His manner was still restrained, but below his calm were the stirrings of a deep agitation. There was tense anxiety in the set of his lips, an inordinate anticipation in the keenness of his eyes. For a space he stood waiting; then, as she made no effort towards response, he stepped to her side.

"Say something!" he exclaimed. "Speak to me! I am waiting for you to speak."

With a low, frightened murmur she drew back, extending her hands, as if to ward him off.

The sound and the movement stung him to action. With a speed that might have been construed into fear, he came still nearer.

"Enid!" he said. "Enid!"

But again she retreated involuntarily.

"Oh, why did you do it?" she exclaimed, suddenly, in a faint, shaken voice. "Oh, why did you do it? Why did you do it?"

For an instant her tone and her manner daunted him; then he straightened his body and raised his head.

"I did it for what is reckoned the most sordid motive in the world," he said, in a level voice. "I did it for money!"

"For money?" With a scared movement she turned upon him, and for the first time since he had made his revelation, he saw her pale, alarmed, incredulous face in the full light of the fire.

"I was wronged!" he said, sharply. "These people had defrauded me. I wanted what was justly mine."

"Wanted?" The word formed itself almost inarticulately.

"Yes; wanted. Wanted with all my might. I have worked, schemed, suffered for this in ways you could never imagine. I thought myself invincible. I believed that if the devil himself stood in my way it would not deter me. And now you — a frail girl — have wrecked the scheme!" He paused again, leaning towards her in sudden unconscious appeal for comprehension.

"I won't say it hasn't been a struggle to come to you like this — to make my confession. It has. My conscience and I have been struggling night and day. I have held out to the last. It was only today — this very day — when I woke to face the crisis of my plans, that I knew I was beaten — knew the fight was over.

"And do you understand why this has happened? Do you know why I am going away as empty-handed as I came? It is because I have seen you — because I love you —"

He put out his hands. But as his fingers touched her, she thrust him away, freeing herself with fierce resentment.

"Don't! don't! don't!" she cried. "You call yourself an impostor — You are worse than that. Much worse. You are a thief!"

He stepped back as though she had struck him, and his hands dropped to his sides.

"Yes, you are a thief!" she said again, hysterically; "a thief!"

The repetition of the word goaded him.

"Wait! Let me defend myself!"

But with a broken sound of protest she flung her hands over her ears.

"No! no! no!" she cried, vehemently. "There is no defence to make. There is no defence. You may leave the money of the sect, but you have stolen things that can never be replaced. Faith — hopes — ideals —" Her voice failed her.

"Mistaken faith — mistaken ideals —" He caught her wrists, drawing her hands downward.

But again she freed herself and confronted him with blazing eyes and a face marred by tears and emotion.

"Nothing is mistaken that lifts one up — that helps one to live. Oh, you don't knew what you have done! You don't know! I thought you so noble — so great — and now —"

"Now I am condemned unheard."

"Unheard? Do you think words could change anything? There is only one thing I wish for now — never, never to see you again as long as either of us live!" With each word her voice rose, and on the last it broke with an excited sob.

While she had been speaking the Prophet's face had become very pale. He turned to her now with a manner that was preternaturally quiet.

"Very well!" he said. "I understand! But there is no need for you to trouble. All our arrangements are made — have been made for months. We attend the Gathering tonight; and afterwards, when Hellier Crescent is quiet, we go — as unobtrusively as we came. You see I give you the key to our plans; you are free to frustrate them, if you think fit. I don't believe I had any real hope of merciful judgment when I came here — women are not merciful when they are robbed of their illusions. But I confess I hoped for justice. I thought that you might hate me —"

"Hate you?" she cried. "Hate you? We only hate what we respect. I don't hate you. I only despise you with all my heart. I want you to go before I despise myself as well!" Her own cruel disillusioning — her own unbearable sense of loss — swept over her afresh; her voice rose again, and again broke hysterically. With an uncontrolled movement of grief and mortification she turned away from him and threw herself upon a couch, burying her face in the pillows.

For several minutes she cried tempestuously; then through the storm of her angry tears she caught the sound of a closing door. With a start she sat up and looked about her.

The faint relic of daylight still showed through the curtains of the window; the firelight still played pleasantly on the untouched tea-table and the fragile furniture; but the room was empty. The Prophet was gone.

CHAPTER VIII

When she realized this fact, Enid rose from her seat with a murmur of dismay. In her sharply feminine sense of loss, she took one involuntary step towards the door; but almost as the step was taken, her anger, her shattered faith assailed her anew, and, with a fresh burst of tears she turned and flung herself back upon the couch.

For a long time she lay with her face among the pillows; then, at last, as her angry sobs died out and the violence of her grief subsided, she sat up, wiped her eyes, and glanced at her dripping handkerchief.

At sight of the handkerchief — a mere wisp of wet cambric — her sense of injury stung her afresh, and once more her lips began to quiver; but fate had decided against further tears. Before her grief had gathered force, the bell of the hall-door sounded once more long and loudly; and hard upon the sound the door of the room opened.

With a start of confusion she sprang to her feet, and turned to confront Norris, standing at a discreet distance, with an apologetic manner and downcast eyes.

"Mr. Bale-Corphew, ma'am," she murmured, as Enid looked at her. "I told him you were not at home; but he said he would wait till whenever he could see you, it didn't matter how long."

With a little cry of dismay and annoyance, Enid put her hands to her disordered hair.

"Oh, how stupid of you!" she cried, tremulously. "You know I can't see him. You know I won't see him. Tell him I'm out — ill — anything you can think of —" But her voice suddenly faltered, and her words ended in a gasp, as she glanced from the servant to the door, which had abruptly reopened, displaying the face and figure of Bale-Corphew himself.

Without hesitation he had entered the room; and without hesitation he walked straight towards her.

"Forgive me!" he exclaimed. "I know this must seem unpardonable; but the occasion is without precedent. May I speak with you alone?"

In the moment of his entry, and during his hurried greeting, Enid had mastered her agitation. She looked at him now with an attempt at calmness.

"Certainly, if you have anything to say."

In the excitement under which he was obviously laboring, he did not observe the coldness of the granted permission. He waited with ill-concealed impatience until Norris had withdrawn, then he turned to her afresh.

"Mrs. Witcherley!" he cried, "you see before you an outraged man!"

He made the announcement fiercely and theatrically; but, to any ear, it would have been evident that, below the instinctive desire for dramatic effect, his voice trembled with genuine agitation — his speech was charged with violent feeling. To Enid, watching him with surprise and curiosity, it was patent at a glance that some circumstance, strange in its occurrence or vital in its issue, had shaken him to the base of his emotional nature. And as she looked at him her own coldness, her own humiliation, suddenly forsook her.

"What is it?" she cried, involuntarily. "What is it? Something has happened?"

For one moment his answer was delayed — held back by the torrent of words that rushed to his lips; then, at last, as his tongue freed itself, he threw out his hands in a fierce gesture.

"Outrage! Outrage and sacrilege!" he cried. "We have been duped — deceived — tricked. We, the Chosen — the Elect!"

"Duped? Deceived?" She echoed the words, faintly. "What do you mean? What has happened?"

"Everything! Everything!" Again he threw out his hands. "This man that we have called Prophet — this man that we have bent the knee to — he is nothing; nothing —" Once more emotion overpowered his words.

"Nothing?" Enid's voice was indistinct, her tongue dry.

" — Nothing but an impostor! An impostor! A thief!"

He spoke loudly — even violently. To his listener it seemed that his voice rang out, filling the room, filling the street outside, filling the whole world. As she had done in the Prophet's presence, she raised her hands and pressed them over her ears. But, even through her fingers, his tones came loud and penetrating.

"An impostor!" he cried, again. "A liar! A blasphemer!"

Her hands dropped from her face.

"Stop! Stop!" she cried, weakly.

But he was beyond appeal.

"You must hear!" he cried. "It is ordained. You have been the unwitting instrument by which the man has fallen."

"I? I? The instrument?" She stared at him with wide eyes and a white face.

"Yes, you!" He stepped to her side. "Without you, suspicion would never have been aroused. Without you, he might have carried out his base designs. It was the power of the Unseen that guided me on the day I entered the Presence Room and found you alone with him." He spoke hurriedly and disjointedly, but as the last word left his lips another expression crossed his face, as though a new suggestion passed through his mind.

"Did you see nothing strange in that Audience?" he demanded. "Did you see nothing strange in the fact that he — a Prophet of Sublime Mysteries — should hold your hand, as any man of the earth might hold it?" He bent still closer, jealousy and suspicion darkening his face.

Enid glanced at him fearfully. "No! No!" she said, sharply. "I — saw nothing strange. He was the Prophet."

Bale-Corphew's face relaxed.

"Ah!" he said, slowly. "I believe you. But, if *you* were blind, *I* saw." He paused and passed his handkerchief over his face. Cold as the day was, drops of perspiration stood upon his forehead.

"I saw. And from that hour the man was lost."

"Lost?"

"Yes, lost." He laughed excitedly; and to Enid the laugh sounded singularly unpleasant, sharp, and cruel. "From that day we have watched him — we, the Six. We have watched him and his friend — the dog who has dared to desecrate the name of Precursor. We have watched them night and day; we have seen them, listened to them hour after hour, while they believed themselves unobserved — ?"

"And what do you know? What have you learned?" There was a strange faintness in the tone of her voice.

"Everything. Only yesterday we touched the key-stone of their scheme. Tonight — this very night — they have planned an escape. They will attend as usual in the Place; they will fool us as they have fooled us before; and then, when the house is quiet — when the Six are at rest, exhausted by prayer and meditation — they will accomplish their vile work. They will plunder the Treasury of the Unseen!"

"Oh no! No!" With a swift movement she turned to him.

He looked at her for an instant, of silence, and then again the unpleasant, excited laugh escaped him.

"You are right," he cried, suddenly. "What you say is right. There will be no plunder. The Treasury of the Unseen will remain inviolate!"

As he paused she made no sound; but her eyes rested upon his, fascinated by their feverish brightness; and in the midst of her silent regard he spoke again, bending forward until his lips approached her ear.

"They have laid their plans," he whispered, with a sudden and savage exultation, "but we also have laid ours. And even we cannot reckon upon the consequences. The spiritual enthusiast is not easy to hold in check, once he has been aroused!"

Enid stared at him, the pupils of her eyes dilated, her lips pale.

"You mean — ? You mean — ?" she stammered; then her fear found voice. "What do you mean?" she demanded, in sharp, alarmed tones.

Bale-Corphew met her question, steadily.

"I mean," he said, with fierce vindictiveness, "that at the Gathering tonight he will be publicly denounced!"

He made the declaration slowly, and each word fell with overwhelming weight upon his companion's understanding. As in the bewildered mazes of a nightmare she saw the crowded chapel, the fanatical, unstable faces of the congregation, the six Arch-Mystics — outraged, incensed, unrelenting; and in their midst the Prophet, tall and grave and masterful, as she had seen him a hundred times. One man facing a sea of ungoverned emotion! At the vision her heart swelled suddenly and her soul sickened. With a gesture, almost as passionate as his own, she turned upon Bale-Corphew.

"You would denounce him before the People?" she said, incredulously. "You would trap him? One man against a hundred! Oh, it would be cowardly! Cruel!"

Bale-Corphew's face flamed to a deeper red.

"Cowardly? Cowardly? Do you know what you are saying? The man is a thief!"

For one moment she shrank before the epithet; the next she raised her head, her eyes flashing, her lips parted.

"You have no right to use that word. You have not seen him steal."

"Seen him? No. But the ears are as reliable as the eyes, and we have heard him declare that he intends to steal."

"Intends! Intends! Intentions are not acts." In her deep agitation, she turned upon him with a new demeanor.

"Oh, be merciful!" she cried. "Give him the benefit of mercy. Wait till the Assembly is over, and then accuse him. If you can prove your accusation, then justice can be done. On the other hand —"

"The other hand?" Again Bale-Corphew's cruel laugh broke from him. "He has not shrunk from lies — from imposture — from blasphemy. Is it likely he will shrink from his reward? Oh no! We will run no risks. The trap has closed. No one will gain access to him tonight until the hour of the Gathering has arrived. It will be my special — my sacred — duty to watch and guard." As he spoke his eyes seemed to devour her face, and before the expression in their depths her strength faltered.

"And why have you come here?" she asked, unsteadily. "Why have you come here? What has this to do with me?"

As she put the questions, he watched her closely; and when her voice quivered, a spasm of emotion — a wave of jealousy and suspicion — swept his face.

"Can you ask that question?" he demanded.

Enid wavered.

"Why not?" she murmured. "Why should I not?"

"Why not?" He laughed again, suddenly and savagely. "Because the man loves you. Because he stole out of the house today — and came here to you. I tracked him here and tracked him back again."

Enid shrank away from him.

"So — so you are a spy?" she said, in a confused, uneven voice.

He turned instantly, his passions aflame.

"A spy?" he cried. "I am a spy? Very well! We will see who comes out victor. The thief or the spy." His voice rose, his face darkened. The demon of jealousy that had pursued him for seven days was free of the leash at last.

"I wanted to know this," he exclaimed. "I wanted to be sure. I had my suspicions, but I wanted proof. On the day I surprised you with him, I suspected; today, when I saw him enter this house, I felt convinced —"

"Convinced of what?"

"Convinced that there is more in this matter than his love for you. That there is also —"

With a swift movement Enid stopped him. She was quivering violently, but she held her head high.

"Yes," she said, distinctly. "Yes, you are quite right. There is more in this matter than his love for me. There is also my love for him!"

Her eyes were blazing; her heart was beating fast. With an agitation equal to Bale-Corphew's own she moved to the fireplace and pressed the bell.

When the servant appeared she turned to her.

"Norris," she said, in a quiet voice, "show Mr. Bale-Corphew out."

CHAPTER IX

There are few phases of human existence more interesting than that in which a young and sensitive woman is compelled by circumstances to cast aside the pleasant artifices, the carefully modulated emotions of a sheltered life, and to face the realities of fact and feeling.

For twenty-three years Enid Witcherley had played with existence — toying with it, enjoying it, as an epicure enjoys a rare wine or a choice morsel of food prepared for his appreciation. Now, as she stood alone in her small drawing-room with its costly decorations, its feminine atmosphere, she was conscious for the first time that the banquet of life is not in reality a display of delicate viands and tempting vintages, but a meal of common bread — sweet or bitter as destiny decrees. She saw this, and with a flash of comprehension knew and acknowledged that her heart and her brain cried out for the wholesome necessary food.

An hour ago, when the Prophet had stood before her and made his confession, she had been overwhelmed by the tide of her own feelings; in the rush of humiliation and disappointment — in the tremendous knowledge that the image she had called gold was in reality but clay — she had been too mortified to see beyond her own horizon. In that moment their places in the drama had been indisputably allotted. She herself had appeared the unoffending heroine, unjustly humiliated in her own eyes and in the eyes of others; he had stood out, in unpardonable guise, the cause — the instrument — of that humiliation. In the bitter knowledge she had confronted him unrelentingly. A spoiled child — an unreasoning feminine egoist.

But now that moment, with its instructive and primitive emotions, was passed by what seemed months — years — a century. By a process of mind as swift as it was subtle, the child had grown into a woman — the egoist had become conscious of another existence. With the entrance of Bale-Corphew — with the sound of her own denunciation upon his lips — a new feeling had awakened within her — a feeling stronger than humiliation, stronger than pride. It had risen, blinding and dazzling her, as a great light might blind and dazzle; and she stood glorified and exalted within its radiance.

As the door had closed upon her second visitor, a long sobbing sigh of excitement, of tumultuous joy and fear shook her from head to foot; she involuntarily drew her figure to its full height, and covered her face with both hands, as though to ward off the light that lay across her world.

But the great moment of joy and comprehension could not last; other and more insistent factors were at work within her mind — claiming, even demanding attention. Almost as the outer door closed upon Bale-Corphew, her hands dropped to her sides and an expression akin to terror crossed her eyes. With a mind rendered supersensitive by its own emotions, she realized what the next five hours might hold; and like a tangible menace the dark, angry face of the Arch-Mystic flashed back upon her consciousness.

While he had been present in the room, while his turbulent voice had filled her ears, she had been only partly alive to the threatened danger; but now that his presence had been removed, now that she was free to sift the meaning of his words, their full significance was borne in upon her. With an alarming clearness of vision, she recognized that behind his threats lay a definite meaning; that the man himself, at all times passionate, and, on occasion, violent in temperament, had suddenly become a danger — something as fierce and menacing as an uncontrolled element.

She realized and understood this rapidly, as only the mind knows and comprehends in moments of stress and crisis; and before her knowledge, all ideas save one fell away like chaff before the wind. At all costs — in face of every obstacle — she must warn and save the Prophet!

With a start of apprehension, she glanced at the clock and saw that the hands marked ten minutes to seven. Moving to the fireplace, she once more pressed the bell; and as Norris answered, turned to her, heedless for perhaps the first time in her life of outward appearances.

"Get me my long black cloak, Norris," she said. "And a black hat and veil. I am going out."

Norris's face expressed no surprise.

"You will be back to dinner, ma'am?" she inquired.

"No. I shall not want dinner. I may not be back till ten — perhaps eleven. If I am late, no one need wait up." She walked to a mirror and began nervously smoothing her ruffled hair, while Norris left the room, and returned with the desired garments.

With the same nervous haste she put on her hat, tied the thick veil over her face, and allowed herself to be helped into her cloak. Then, without a word, she crossed the drawing-room, passed through the hall of the flat, and entered the lift.

At the street-door she was compelled to wait while the hall-porter called a cab; and the momentary delay almost overtaxed her patience. An audible sound of relief escaped her when the clatter of hoofs and jingle of bells announced that the wait was over.

"St. George's Terrace!" she ordered, in a low voice, and it seemed to her perturbed mind that even the stolid attendant must find something portentous in the words; then she sank into the corner of the cab and closed her eyes, as she heard her order repeated to the cabman, and felt the horse swing forward into the stream of traffic.

More than once she altered her position as the distance between Knightsbridge and St. George's Terrace lessened. She was devoured by impatience and yet paralyzed by dread. Once, as the cab halted in a block of traffic, she heard a clock strike seven, and at the sound the blood rushed to her face as she thought of the nearness of her ordeal; but an instant later she drew out her watch to verify the time, and paled with sudden apprehension as she realized that the clock was slow.

So her mind oscillated until the cab drew up beside the curb; and, with a nervous start, she heard the cabman open the trap-door.

"What number, lady?" he asked.

She answered almost guiltily: "No number! Just stop here! Put me down here!" She rose, gathering her long cloak about her.

Try as she might, she could not control her excitement, as she crossed the roadway and entered Hellier Crescent after a week's absence. Her hand was trembling as she raised the heavy knocker on the familiar door; and her voice shook as she repeated the necessary formula.

There was a slight delay — a slight hesitancy on the part of the door-keeper; then the slide, which had opened at her knock, closed with a click, and the massive door swung back.

She stepped forward eagerly, but on the moment that she entered the hall her heart sank. With a thrill of apprehension she saw that in place of the humble member of the congregation who usually attended there, the tall, fair-bearded Arch-Mystic known as George Norov was guarding the door. Small though the incident might appear, it conveyed to her, as no spoken declaration could have done, the spirit of action and vigilance reigning in the House.

While the thought flashed through her mind, Norov surveyed her from his great height.

"You are in good time, my child; the Gathering is for eight o'clock."

She looked up at him.

"Yes," she said, quickly. "I know it is for eight o'clock, but I have come early. I have come because I wish —" Her courage faltered before the intent, searching gaze of his blue eyes.

"I have come," she added, with gathered resolution, "because I desire private Audience with the Prophet — because there is something on my Soul of which I must unburden myself."

The Arch-Mystic looked at her and his eyes seemed cold as steel.

"The Prophet holds private Audience only in the morning," he replied, in an even voice.

Enid flushed.

"I know that. But there are exceptions to the rule —"

The Arch-Mystic shook his head.

"The Prophet holds private Audience only in the morning."

"But the Prophet is generous. Five minutes alone with him will satisfy me — three minutes — two minutes —" Her tone quickened as her anxiety increased.

Still Norov's blue eyes met hers unswervingly.

"The Prophet holds private Audience only in the morning."

At the second repetition her apprehension rose to fear; and in her alarmed trepidation she conceived a new idea. With a rapid searching glance her eyes travelled over the Arch-Mystic's powerful figure, while she mentally measured his physical strength with that of the Prophet. Her survey was short and comprehensive; and her decision came with equal speed. With a subtle change of manner and voice she made a fresh appeal. Turning to him with a gesture of deference, she spoke again in a soft and conciliatory voice.

"Of course, you are right in what you say," she murmured. "But I am going to make an appeal. If I may not see the Prophet in private Audience, then let me see him in your presence! I have only a dozen words to say; and, if necessary, I will say them in your presence. You can see it is urgent, when I am willing to humiliate myself. It is only for her Soul that a woman will conquer her pride. You won't deny peace to my Soul?" Her voice dropped, her whole expression pleaded.

For a moment — for just one moment — it seemed to her desperate gaze that his hard blue eyes softened; the next, their cold, unyielding glance disillusioned her of hope.

"It is useless to appeal to me," he said; "but if you very much desire it, you can make your request to my brother Mystic — Horatio Bale-Corphew. He is guarding the Prophet's Threshold."

Whether the man had any glimmering of knowledge as to her private connection with Bale-Corphew and the Prophet was not to be read from his austere face. His words might have been spoken in all innocence, or might have been spoken deliberately and with malice. But in either case the result, so far as his listener was concerned, was the same. A sense of frightened impotence fell upon her — a knowledge that her enemy had a longer reach and a more powerful arm than she had guessed.

By a great effort she controlled her feelings.

"Thank you!" she said, quietly, "but I will not trouble Mr. Bale-Corphew. If I may, I will wait in the Place until the Gathering is assembled."

Her companion bent his head.

"Permission is granted!" he said.

For a moment longer she stood, burning with apprehensive dread. On one hand was the Prophet — trapped and unaware of his peril; on the other was Bale-Corphew — implacable, enraged, unrelaxing in his pursuit. She waited irresolute, until the cold, inquiring gaze of the Arch-Mystic made action compulsory; then, scarcely conscious of the movement, she inclined her head in mechanical acknowledgment of his courtesy, and, turning away, passed down the lofty, sombre hall.

Never in after-life was she able to remember, with any degree of distinctness, her threading of the familiar corridors leading to the chapel. Her consciousness of outer things was numbed by mental strife. Reaching the heavy curtain that shut off the sacred precinct, she thrust it aside with nervous impetuosity and stood looking around the deserted chapel — glancing from the rows of empty chairs to the Sanctuary, where the great golden Throne stood shrouded in a white cloth, and the silver censers lay awaiting the flame.

At a first glance it seemed that the chapel was entirely empty, but as her eyes grew accustomed to the modulated light diffused by eight large tapers, she saw that the Sanctuary was occupied by one sombre figure that flitted silently between the lectern and the Throne. For an instant her heart leaped, for the man was of the same height and build as the Precursor; but a second glance put her hopes to flight. The Mystic within the Sanctuary was the humble member of the congregation whose duty it was to wait upon the Prophet.

As she passed slowly and automatically up the aisle, the man turned and looked at her; but after a cursory glance returned to his task of setting the Sanctuary in order.

The look and the evident unconcern chilled and daunted her anew. With a movement of despair she paused, and sank into one of the empty chairs.

For a space that seemed eternal, she sat huddled in her seat — her hands clasped nervously in her lap; her ears alert to catch the slightest sound; her eyes unconsciously following the movements of the man within the Sanctuary; then, suddenly and abruptly, the tension snapped; and action — action of some description — became imperative. She rose from her seat.

After she had risen, she stood aimlessly looking about her at the black-and-white walls, at the rows of chairs, at the gleaming octagonal symbol that hung from the roof; then, as if magnetically attracted, her glance travelled back to the man inside the Sanctuary rail.

There was nothing remarkable in the spare figure, moving reverently from one sacred object to another; but as her eyes rested on the colorless, ascetic face, her own cheeks flushed with a new hope — a new inspiration. With a quick movement she glanced furtively behind her; and, stepping carefully between the chairs, regained the aisle and moved swiftly and noiselessly up the chapel.

Her heart was beating so fast, the nervous strain was so intense, that when she reached the railing she stood for a moment unable to command her voice. And when the Mystic — becoming suddenly aware of her near presence — turned and confronted her, a faint sound of nervous alarm slipped from her.

For a space the two looked at each other; and at last the man appeared to realize that something was expected of him. Bending his head, he uttered the formula of the sect.

"In what can I serve you?"

The familiar words braced Enid. She glanced at him afresh, and in that glance her plan of action arranged itself. For one moment, as she had walked up the aisle, her hand had sought her purse, but now, as she scanned the ascetic face of this unworldly servant, her fingers involuntarily loosened and the purse slipped back into her pocket. With a new resolve, she looked him straight in the eyes.

"You can do me a great service — a very great service," she said, quietly, in her soft, clear voice.

The man looked at her in slow inquiry.

"Oh, I know you are surprised," she added, quickly. "I know this seems unusual —" She paused in momentary hesitation.

The Mystic appeared distressed.

"My — my duty —" he broke in, uneasily. "My duty is to —"

But she checked him suddenly.

"Charity is greater than duty!" she said, in a low, impressive tone. By the same feminine intuition that had made her discard her purse, she saw that by a semi-mystical appeal — and by that alone — could she hope to succeed. Laying her hands upon the Sanctuary railing, she leaned forward, and raised her large eyes to the man's face.

"Which do *you* consider the greater virtue?" she asked. "Duty or charity?"

The Mystic looked at her.

"Charity," he said, at last, hesitatingly, "the Prophet teaches us —"

Enid's face flushed.

"Yes! yes!" she cried. "The Prophet teaches us that charity is the greater virtue. He tells us that we are to rely upon ourselves — and also upon each other. We are to help ourselves — and to help each other." Her voice shook, her face glowed in her excitement and suspense.

"I am in need of help," she added. "In desperate need. And you can help me."

Her tone was urgent, her compelling gaze never faltered. She knew that this was her last chance — that, if this man failed her, catastrophe was inevitable.

The Mystic stirred uncomfortably, and his glance turned half fearfully from the intent, appealing face to the lectern on which rested the white-bound Scitsym.

With a sudden access of enthusiasm, Enid spoke again.

"There is something troubling my Soul," she said. "Something that I must confess to the Prophet tonight. My whole happiness — all my peace — depends upon confessing it. I cannot speak with him before the Gathering assembles; but I can write my confession. Will you save my Soul? Will you carry my confession to him?"

Until the words were actually spoken, she did not realize how immensely she had staked upon her chances of success. In a fever of anxiety she waited, watching the man's gaze as it wavered undecidedly over the Scitsym, then returned, as if magnetized, to her face.

"In twenty minutes the Gathering will be assembled," he murmured.

"I know, I know. But there is still time. It is a matter of — of faith — of peace of mind."

The man shuffled his feet.

"It — it is impossible," he said.

"Why impossible?"

"Because the Prophet is exalted tonight. The Arch-Mystics themselves are guarding the Threshold. The Prophet is exalted; he must not be disturbed."

"But if it is necessary to disturb him? If there is a Soul in danger?"

"The Prophet must not be disturbed. What are we, that we should thrust our wrong-doing or our sorrow upon the Mighty One?"

At the words a rage of apprehension shook Enid. She lifted her head, and her fingers closed fiercely round the iron bar that topped the railing.

"Silence!" she said, excitedly. "You do not know what you are saying! The Prophet sets his people high above himself. The message of a Soul in distress is of more value in his eyes than a hundred moments of exaltation. Take care that his wrath does not fall upon you!"

Involuntarily the man paled.

"Yes. Take care!" she cried. "Take care! You have the well-being — the whole future — of one Soul in your hands tonight. How will you answer to the Prophet, if you fail in the trust?"

The Mystic cowered.

"If you fail, the wrong can never be repaired. And the doing of the action will cost you nothing. Take this note —" With agitated haste she tore a leaf from a tiny note-book that hung at her waist. "Take this note. Tell no one. Give it into the Prophet's own hands —" She drew out a pencil and wrote a few enigmatical words. "Give it into his own hands; and I can promise you that your reward will be greater than you think." With a rapid movement, she roiled up the paper and held it out to him.

"Take it," she said, impressively. "And remember that it is

something important, essential — sacred." On the last word her voice rose; then, without warning, it suddenly broke.

A curtain at the back of the Sanctuary had been drawn aside; and for the second time that evening, the face of Bale-Corphew confronted her through the dusk.

CHAPTER X

For one instant Enid stood spellbound; then involuntarily she stepped backward, crumpling the slip of paper in her hand.

At the same movement Bale-Corphew advanced and, passing the Mystic, indicated the Sanctuary curtain.

"Go!" he commanded, in an unsteady voice. And as the man slunk away, he wheeled round and confronted Enid.

"So this is your action?" he said, tremulously. "This is your conception of honor? Truly, woman is the undoing of man!" With an excited gesture, he lifted his hand and extended it towards the white Scitsym lying upon the lectern.

But Enid met his attack with the courage that sometimes outlives hope.

"A just man need fear no woman!" she exclaimed. "It is because you are unjust and a coward that you fear — that you suspect — that you find it necessary to hide and spy."

The color surged over his face.

"I have been outraged!" he cried — "I have been outraged!"

"And, like an unreasoning animal, you turn to devour the thing that has hurt you?"

"I demand justice."

She threw out her hands and laughed suddenly and hysterically.

"And you call this justice? You call it justice to trap one man and set a hundred others loose upon him?"

But Bale-Corphew turned upon her.

"And what is this man to you?" he cried. "What spell has he cast upon you that you can forget his outrage and his blasphemy?"

Enid met the question with her new fortitude; searching Bale-Corphew's turbulent face, she answered with a certain high simplicity.

"I do not know," she said. "Once I believed that I admired him — that I looked up to him — because he was a Prophet; something higher and better than myself. Now I know that my belief was wrong and false; that it was because he is a man — because, before everything else in the world, he is a man — that I turned to him, that I relied upon him."

Bale-Corphew gave a short, cruel laugh.

"So that is it? That is the secret? He is a man? Well, I will strip him of his manhood! We have had our disillusioning; yours is to come. Here, on this sacred spot where he has been so exalted, he will bite the dust."

He paused triumphantly; and in the pause there rose again to Enid's mind the picture of one tall, white-robed figure confronting a sea of faces — all incensed — all passionately, vindictively unanimous in desire.

"Oh no!" she said, suddenly, faltering before the picture. "No! No! You cannot. You must not. Be merciful! Let him go. And if there is anything — any recompense —" But even as it was spoken, the appeal died. Somewhere in the heart of the House a solemn clock chimed the hour of eight; and as though the sound were a signal, the curtain of the chapel door was drawn softly back, and a stream of dark-robed figures poured over the empty floor.

For a moment she stood immovable before the imminence of the crucial scene; then, with a sensation of physical weakness and helplessness, she turned, moved blindly forward, and sank into a vacant seat.

At the same moment Bale-Corphew left her without a word, and passed rapidly down the aisle.

Great fear frequently exercises a paralyzing effect upon the body. With the undeniable knowledge that the time for action — the time for hope — was irrevocably passed, Enid felt deprived of the power to move. She sat crouching in her seat, every sense alive and strained, but with limbs that were overpowered and weighted as if by tangible fetters.

Thrilling to this numb and impotent sense of dread, she heard the devotees enter the chapel, one after another, and pass to their chosen seats with soft, gliding steps. With a sickening knowledge of approaching catastrophe, she saw another of the unconventional black-robed servants emerge from behind the Sanctuary curtain, and proceed with maddening deliberation to light the sixteen groups of wax tapers that were set at intervals along the walls. Mechanically her eyes followed the man's movements; and it seemed that each new taper that spat, flickered, and shot up into a light was a symbol, a portent of the scene to come.

As the last candle was lighted, the shuffling of feet and the stir of garments that, since the entry of the first devotee, had unceasingly filled the chapel suddenly subsided, and nerved to motion by the lull, she turned and glanced behind her.

The scene, familiar though it was, impressed her anew. It was a strange effect in black and white. The black clothes of the congregation seemed massed together in a sombre blur; their strained, fanatical faces looked white and set; while the marble walls shone out, sharp and polished, in the same contrasting hues. Over the whole scene the concentrated light and accentuated shadow thrown by the great sconces glowing with tapers, made a variation of tone almost as vivid as that seen on a moonlight night.

Unconsciously she recognized the curious, the almost barbaric picturesqueness of light and grouping; but her eyes had barely skimmed the scene when the meaning of the hush that filled the place was brought home to her mind.

Glancing towards the curtain that hid the entrance, she saw the figure of the Prophet move slowly into the chapel and pass up the aisle, attended by the Precursor and the Six Arch-Mystics.

He moved forward with grave, dignified steps, and with a head held even higher than usual, and reaching the Sanctuary gate, passed through it without hesitation.

The action was so calm — so natural — so like what she had witnessed night after night — that Enid sat newly petrified, her senses striving to associate this strong figure with the man who, only a few hours before, had humiliated himself in her presence. For a moment her mind refused the connection of ideas; but the next a full realization of the position swept over her, galvanizing her mentally and physically, as she turned in her seat and glanced at the seven who were following in the wake.

First behind his master came the Precursor. And to Enid's searching gaze it seemed that his face was set into unfamiliar and anxious lines; but under his black cap and red hair, his skin looked colorless and drawn. But after the first glance, her eyes were not for him; with swift apprehension they passed to the six Arch-Mystics who, walking two and two, formed the procession.

Animated by the speed of actual fear, her gaze passed from the abnormally agitated face of old Arian, the blind Arch-Councillor, to the dark, turbulent face of Bale-Corphew, who brought up the rear. The survey was rapid and comprehensive; and to her uneasy mind the thought came with unerring certainty that, on all the six faces — differing so markedly in physical characteristics — there was a common look of suppressed excitement, of suppressed resolve.

As they passed her seat, Norov turned and shot a glance of cold curiosity in her direction; but otherwise the whole group seemed unaware of her presence. Still inert, she sat, watching every movement in the scene before her as one might watch a drama that would, at a given moment, cease to be entertainment and become real life.

Very quietly the Prophet advanced to the Scitsym and, following the customary routine, opened it and began to read.

The words were a strange jargon of mystical counsel interspersed with the relation of mystical visions and ecstasies. On ordinary lips, the long, disjointed sentences and disconnected phrases would have sounded vague and incomprehensible; but, from the first, it had been one of the Prophet's special gifts that his deep, grave voice could lend weight and meaning to the fantastic utterances. And tonight it seemed that he intended to put forth all his powers; for scarcely had he opened the book and begun to read, than a stir of interest passed over the congregation; and even Enid, enmeshed in her own terrors, bent forward involuntarily.

He spoke very slowly, enunciating every word with studied seriousness; and from time to time he paused and looked across the sea of fixed and almost adoring faces turned in his direction. It was as if, by strength of will, he had determined that no point, no syllable, of this, his last reading, should be lost upon his hearers. More than once, Bale-Corphew moved uneasily and shot a glance at Norov; but the Prophet was unconscious of these surreptitious signs.

For half an hour he read on, slowly, distinctly, impressively; then, still following the routine of the evening service, he closed the book and calmly moved across the Sanctuary to the Throne. As he neared it, the Precursor stepped forward deferentially and conducted him to the foot of the gilt steps.

Having ascended, he took his seat with calm impassivity and, resting his hands upon the arms of the great gold chair, looked out once more upon the massed faces. This, according to custom, was the signal for a general movement. The congregation swayed forward, prostrating themselves upon the ground, while the Arch-Mystics gathered their wide, black robes about them and assumed attitudes of rapt contemplation.

In obedience to usage, Enid also dropped upon her knees and covered her face with her hands. But though her pose was conventional, there was little place in her thoughts for either prayer or meditation. One idea — and one only — absorbed her being. How, and at what moment, must she gather strength to act? She crouched upon the ground, her hands pressed tightly over her eyes. It seemed to her that all the torture, all the suspense and apprehension of the universe, were gathered into that half-hour of appalling silence. Once she ventured to unlace her fingers and glance through them fearfully; but at sight of the Prophet, calm, impassive, unconscious of his threatened danger — at sight of the six sombre shrouded figures that sat inside the Sanctuary railing, her blood turned cold and her courage quailed.

When the sign that ended the evening's meditation was given, she rose with the rest and sank weakly into her seat. Then, in dumb, stricken helplessness such as envelops us in a terrible dream, she saw the Prophet rise very slowly and stand on the steps of the Throne, looking solemnly down upon the people.

During his change of position, she sat vacillating pitiably. The knowledge that in a single moment he would have begun to speak spurred her to a fever of alarm, while a terrible nervous incapacity chained her limbs and paralyzed her tongue.

Bale-Corphew's words rose to her mind. "He will fool us — as he has fooled us before." In the apprehension aroused by the memory, she half rose in her chair, her hands grasping the back of the seat in front of her; but suddenly the chapel, the lights, the congregation seemed to fade from her vision, and she sank back into her place. The Prophet had begun to speak.

"My People," he said, very calmly and distinctly, "heretofore I have spoken to you as a teacher. Tonight I will speak to you as one of yourselves."

Something in the tone — something in the words — struck a note of surprise and uneasiness. Again Bale-Corphew shot a swift glance at Norov, and old Michael Arian lifted his head and strained his sightless eyes towards the Throne, while Enid's hands tightened spasmodically on the back of the chair in front of her, and her lips parted in new fear. What was he going to say? How much further was he going to compromise himself? But the body of the congregation swayed forward in absorbed attention, and the Prophet continued to survey the fixed faces with grave, steady eyes.

"My People," he said, "you are an unusual gathering. Some would call you a gathering of fanatics — some might even call you a gathering of fools. But fools, fanatics, or Mystics, you are all men and women. You are all human beings!"

Old Arian started, and Norov's cold, blue eyes flashed; but still the Prophet was oblivious of their emotion.

"It is always well to study one's own kind; and tonight I am going to speak to you of a man. I am going to tell you the story of a man — a man as passionate, as headstrong, as weak and vulnerable as you yourselves." He halted for a moment, and his glance seemed to grow more concentrated, more intense.

"Once, many years ago, there was a boy born here, in this city of London. Don't lose patience! My story has the merit of truth.

"There was nothing pleasant, there was nothing easy, in the circumstances of this boy's birth. His first sight of the world was gained through the window of a tenement-house, and the picture he saw was the picture of an alley — dark, foul, teeming with life. His first knowledge of existence was the realization of poverty — not the free, wholesome poverty of the country, but the grinding, sordid, continuous poverty of the town, that no tongue can adequately describe.

"These were his surroundings — this was his environment; and yet — so great are the miracles that love can accomplish —

every day of that boy's life was illumined and glorified by one presence. God in his bounty had given him a mother!"

It was the first time in any discourse that he had mentioned the supreme Name, and as if conscious of the tremor it aroused, he continued his narrative without pause.

"To say that a boy's life is made happier by his mother's existence sounds too trite and obvious to bear any weight; but it is through the obvious facts of life that the world's machinery is kept in motion. The inexpressible, unwearying tenderness of this mother for her son, the love of this boy for his mother, grew with the passage of time — grew into something so significant, so vital and so deep, that even the poisonous atmosphere of the alley could not thwart its growth.

"This feeling grew in the boy's heart; and with it — by a necessary law of nature — another feeling took root and grew also. Fired by stories of a past, in which wealth and position had been won by his forefathers, he conceived the idea of becoming in his own person a hero — a knight-errant. And in the grimy, common alley; in the poor, bare sitting-room where his mother sewed unendingly; in the dark closet under the slates where at night he dreamed his child's dreams, he built castles such as never stood upon the hills of Spain!

"The germ of his ambition fell into his soul like a seed of fire; and, like a seed of fire, sprang into a flame. At whatever price — at whatever sacrifice — there must be a golden future, in which the mother he adored would sit in high places; in which the worn hands would never ply a needle except for pastime, the frail figure grow straight and strong, the pale face warm and brighten with the colors of health!

"It was a very humble, a very young ambition, but it sprang from the true, clean source of untainted love, like which there is nothing else in all the world." He paused; and from his grave voice it seemed that a wave of emotion passed across the chapel. The congregation, too fascinated by his words to question their meaning, drew a sigh of rapt anticipation. Enid, amazed, bewildered, moved beyond herself, sat immovable — her face pale, her great eyes fixed upon the Throne. Only the six Arch-Mystics stirred uneasily, glancing at each other with quiet, uncertain looks.

Presently, as though he had marshalled his ideas for the continuation of his speech, the Prophet raised his hand.

"My People," he began, again, "do not think that I am going to compel you to listen to a psychological discourse upon this boy's development. That is not my intention. But were I to hold up a picture for your inspection, you could not properly appreciate it were you ignorant of the art of drawing. And so it is with my story. To understand the completed work, you must understand the manner of its growth.

"Though this boy lived in obscurity, he was bound by one link with the great things of the world. But for the unjust disinheritance of his father, he would have been heir to a vast property; and through all his youth, this had been the golden mirage that had floated before his vision — this had been the fabled country from which his castle rose. Steadily, unfalteringly, one idea had expanded in his mind. By some brave action — by some deed of heroism — he was to win back the lost inheritance.

"Time passed. And with its passage the wheel of fate revolved. By one of those strange chances for which no man can account, the opportunity that the boy longed for fell across his path.

"It came. But it came enveloped in no cloud of glory. The path to the lost inheritance was steep and rugged and dark. He was called upon to leave his mother; to leave the place that, however sordid, however mean, was yet his home; and to enter upon a period of servitude with an unknown master — a man related to him by blood, whom report described as an eccentric — a miser — a madman."

As he said these words a curious thing occurred. A wave of color flushed old Arian's sightless face; an inarticulate sound escaped him, and he made a tremulous attempt to rise. But the movement was instantly checked by Bale-Corphew, who bent close to him and whispered quickly in his ear.

Neither gesture nor whisper was noted by the Prophet. His own face had paled as if with some deep emotion; and lowering his raised hand, he spoke again with a new, suppressed intensity.

"Then began the vital period of that boy's career. He left his home — he left the mother he loved — he went into voluntary exile, animated by one purpose. Remember that, my People! He went into the service of this man animated by one purpose — the determination to win back his rightful fortune! And for seven weary years he continued his pursuit. For the seven most vital years of his youth he suppressed every instinct that animates a boy!

"He worked more laboriously than the laborer in the fields, for mental servitude is more galling to the young than any physical strain. But he never faltered; and at last he had the pride of knowing that his end was gained — he had the pride of knowing that he had become indispensable to the master whom he served!" Again he paused, but this time the pause was of impressive weight. Unconsciously, and without analyzing the feeling, every member of the congregation felt that some announcement was pending — that some extraordinary revelation was about to be made.

Enid sat rigid, holding her breath in an agony of suspense, fascinated and appalled by the incomprehensible discourse. Behind the high railing, old Michael Arian's lips moved rapidly and nervously, as though he were muttering inaudible prayers; while Bale-Corphew's florid face flamed, as, with a rapid, agitated movement, he glanced over the tense faces of the congregation. For one moment it seemed that he was bracing himself for action, but before his intentions could bear fruit, the voice of the Prophet again rang out across the chapel.

"My People!" he said. "It is now that I appeal to your humanity! It is now that I ask each one of you — men and women — to stand in this boy's place — this boy, built like yourselves of human desires, human hopes, human weaknesses. After seven long years he touched the knowledge that he had become indispensable; and the bearer of that knowledge was Death — his master's master!

"Death came; and in his chill presence the boy saw his task completed — laid aside like a written scroll!

"It was the most glorious moment of his life — that moment in which he stood with unshaken faith, looking towards the future. But the darker side of existence was his portion; he had been born to the darker side. Within one hour of his master's death, his dreams were dispelled. He learned that, in the eyes of the man he had served, he had never passed beyond the position of the outcast — the dependent, whose services are liberally rewarded by the gift of a few hundred pounds. The fortune — the inheritance — the golden mirage, was no longer existent, save as something that did not concern him. By the disposition of his master's will, it had passed into the coffers of a religious body — a fantastic, unknown sect to which the old man had belonged!"

The announcement fell with strange effect. Enid, inspired by sudden terror, rose to her feet; Bale-Corphew sat gripping the arm of his chair, his face contorted, his mouth working, while a rustle, an audible murmur of excitement passed over the whole chapel, and the Precursor, who all along had been crouching at the foot of the throne, turned quickly and anxiously towards his master.

But the Prophet reassured him by a gesture. It seemed that he was exalted by some emotion, lifted above his surroundings by some invisible power.

"Put yourselves in this boy's place!" he cried. "Was there ever a position so intensely human? The thing he had striven for — the thing he needed inordinately — had been wrenched from him by a band of people who, in his eyes, were either fools or knaves. What would you have done in his position? What would have been your impulse? What your instinct? If I know anything of human nature, it would have been the same as his — precisely, accurately the same as his!

"He had known for years of this sect to which his master belonged; and for years he had held it in contempt. In his normal, youthful eyes, the idea of a creed that denied the high, simple theory of Christianity, and awaited the coming of a mythical Prophet was a subject for healthy scorn. And now suddenly it was forced upon his understanding that this anæmic sect — this mystical, anticipated Prophet — were his rivals — the despoilers of his private intimate hopes.

"Such a knowledge has power to work a miracle; and in one single night it changed this boy into a man. Embittered, hopeless, stranded, inspiration came to him. He conceived the tremendous idea of entering upon a new fight — a second quest of the great inheritance. He conceived the idea; and standing, as it were, upon a different plane of life, he saw —"

But the Prophet got no further. With a gesture of violent excitement, Bale-Corphew rose; at the same instant the Precursor sprang to his feet and stood in a defensive attitude before the Throne.

The whole scene was enacted in a second. Enid, grasping its full meaning, turned very white and dropped back into her seat, while the whole congregation strained forward in unanimous amazement and curiosity.

And then, for the first time, the hot, angry glance of Bale-Corphew met that of the Prophet. He glared at him for one moment in speechless rage, then he turned to the people.

"Mystics!" he cried, in a choked voice. "In accordance with a solemn duty, I — I proclaim this man to be —"

But before he could proceed the Precursor interrupted.

"People! Mystics!" he cried, raising his penetrating voice. "Is this right? Is this permissible?"

A murmur rose from the chapel.

Bale-Corphew's face became purple.

"People! hear me!" he exclaimed. "This man is no Prophet. He is an impostor! A fraud! I have proof. I can give you proof!"

Of the extraordinary effect of these words Enid — crouching helplessly in her seat — saw nothing. All her senses were riveted upon one object — the tall, calm figure upon the steps of the Throne. By the power of intuition, rather than by physical obser-vation, she saw the look of intense surprise, of incredulity merging to dismay, that crossed the Prophet's face at the Arch-Mystic's words. And at the sight the real meaning of his incomprehensible discourse passed over her mind in a wave of incredulous admira-tion. Believing himself secure in his position, he had voluntarily chosen to denounce himself.

That was her first thought as the matter became clear to her; but a chilling second thought followed sharp upon it. What would be the Prophet's reading of Bale-Corphew's knowledge? Would not one solution — and one only — present itself to his mind? The idea that she had betrayed his confidence. With the horror of the suggestion an ungovernable impulse filled her — an impulse to rise — to go to him — sweep the doubt from his mind. But an instant later the merely egotistical thought was obliterated by the greater issues that filled the moment.

After Bale-Corphew had spoken an uproar — a clamor — had suddenly filled the chapel; and now the rapt concourse of people had become as a turbulent sea. The Precursor, pale with intense nervous excitement, stood vainly striving to make his voice heard; while Bale-Corphew, closely surrounded by his fellow-Mystics, gesticulated violently.

At last the Prophet raised his hand; and by habit and training, the people subsided into silence.

Instantly Bale-Corphew's voice rang out.

"Listen!" he cried; "listen!"

But again the Precursor interrupted.

"People," he demanded, "will you refuse the Prophet the right of speech? Will you refuse to hear the Prophet's words?"

"This is sacrilege! Sacrilege!" Norov suddenly raised his voice. "Listen to your Councillor!"

"Listen to the Prophet! The Voice of the Prophet calls upon you. Will you deny it?" The Precursor's voice shook with excitement.

"This is the truth! I tell you the truth!" Bale-Corphew appealed to the people with out-stretched arms.

But the tumult broke forth again.

"Mystics! Mystics!" Old Arian's shrill, alarmed tones rose for an instant, only to be drowned in the clamor.

Then out of the confused babel of sound one cry became distinguishable.

"The Prophet! The Prophet! Let the Prophet speak!"

For a space confusion reigned; then, answering to the demand, the Prophet again lifted his right hand.

As though it exercised some potent spell, his calm, imperious gesture subdued the turmoil. When silence had been restored he began to speak; and never, since he had addressed the first Gathering, had so deep a note of domination and decision been audible in his voice.

"Mystics!" he cried, "there is no time for preamble or delay. As the Arch-Mystic says, you must have truth! Perhaps there is no need to tell you that the history I have just related to you has an imminent bearing upon your lives and mine. You probably know, without my telling, that the boy of my story and I are one and the same person; that the fanatic sect, for which I was made a beggar, is your own sect — the sect of the Mystics. But so it is. On a wild, dark night ten years ago I learned that the money which should have been mine — the money which should have been the recompense for my mother's hard life — had been given to you. Given for the use of a Prophet in whose coming you believed!

"My feelings on that night were the criminal feelings that underlie all civilization. I had only one desire — to destroy — to be avenged. My uncle, Andrew Henderson, was an Arch-Mystic of your sect; and on the night he died, your sacred Scitsym was in his house!"

The congregation thrilled, and the blind Arch-Councillor turned and clutched Bale-Corphew's arm.

"My first impulse was to destroy that book. Look at it, look at it!" He pointed to the lectern. "Ten years ago, I knelt before a fire with its pages in my hand, and black thoughts of revenge in my heart. But the devil of temptation lurks in strange places. In the very act of destruction, an inspiration came to me. A man was expected! A Prophet was expected! And in the pages of the Scitsym were contained the attributes, the secret signs, the manifold ways in which he was to make good his claim.

"I come of an obstinate stock — of a stock that in the past has overcome many obstacles. That night I copied out the whole of your Scitsym, and afterwards, as soon as I reasonably could, I left Scotland.

"I went at once to my mother; I told her that, according to the disposition of my uncle's will, I was to inherit his fortune in ten years' time, and that in the interval I was to fit myself for wealth by profound study. It was the first time in all my life that I had lied to her!

"But to come to the end, your Prophet was to be a student of

Eastern lore. With this knowledge in my mind, I started with my mother for the East. What has happened since then is immaterial. My second probation has been as hard as my first. But I accomplished two things. I fitted myself mentally and physically for the part I was going to play, and I made one stanch, wholly disinterested friend!" With a gesture of grave affection, he indicated the Precursor.

In the opportunity that the slight pause gave, Bale-Corphew sprang forward and, resting his hands upon the Sanctuary railing, faced the congregation.

"People!" he cried, hoarsely, "be not deceived! This man pretends to tell you what he is. He is blinding you — weaving a bandage of specious words across your eyes. But I will undeceive you. I will tear the bandage —" He hesitated, stammered, paused.

With a movement full of fire, full of authority, the Prophet stepped from the Throne.

"Silence!" he cried. "There is no need for interference. This matter is between the People and myself." With a pale face and burning eyes he stepped forward, and standing beside the Arch-Mystic confronted the congregation.

"I will tell you everything that this man would tell you," he said, in a steady voice. "I believe I will even use the word he himself would choose. I am a thief! I am a thief — in intention if not in act!"

The effect of the word was tremendous. A perfectly audible gasp went up from the breathless crowd; and, by one accord, the people rose and swayed upward towards the Sanctuary.

Calm and immovable as a rock, the Prophet held his place.

"Yes," he said, steadily, "until this morning I have virtually been a thief. Until this morning it was my firm intention to take by force that which should have come to me as my right. The fact that my intention faltered at the last moment does not affect the case. I wish to make no appeal. My desire" — his voice suddenly quickened — "my desire is plainly and simply to state my case.

"Morally I have done you no wrong. My teaching has been the expounding of simple truths, that my personal action could not desecrate. I stand before you tonight empty-handed as I came.

The one thing I claim from you is judgment!

"Judge me! I am in your hands. If you think I deserve punishment, punish me! If you think circumstances have made me what I am, then stand aside! Let me pass out of your lives!"

There was a great silence; then a woman's sharp cry rang out across the chapel, as, with a savage movement, three of the Arch-Mystics sprang upon the Prophet.

"Sacrilege! Sacrilege!" Bale-Corphew's voice rose loud and violent.

But he had calculated without his host. The fanaticism of a crowd is a dangerous weapon with which to tamper, and the dethronement of a king is not accomplished in a day. With the speed of light, the element he had unloosed turned upon himself.

Again one word disentangled itself from the medley of sounds.

"The Prophet! The Prophet!" Like an ignited fuse, instinct had been lighted in the people. The man who for months had been exalted — honored — well-nigh worshipped — was in imminent peril! That one thought submerged and demolished every other.

There was a forward movement — a roar — a crash — and the high, gilt railings of the Sanctuary went down as before a storm.

To Enid, who had been borne irresistibly upward on the human tide, there was one overpowering moment of fear and clamor, in which the cry of "The Prophet! The Prophet!" dominated her consciousness; then, to her, the world became suddenly and mercifully sightless, soundless, and void.

*****

When at last her eyes opened — when at last her senses falteringly returned to the consciousness of present things — she was in her own familiar room. The atmosphere breathed of repose and peace; through the drawn curtains the hum of London came subdued and soothing; in the room itself the lights were modulated and the fire glowed soft and mellow, while a faint, pungent smell of restoratives filled the air. But these details came but vaguely to her appreciation, for the first object upon which her glance and her ideas rested was the figure of John Henderson, kneeling beside the couch on which she lay.

For a long, silent space she gazed bewildered into the grave face bent over her own — striving to fathom whether this was another phase of an extraordinarily prolonged and harassing dream, or whether it had any bearing upon real life; then, as the pained, bewildered sensation deepened in her mind, it was suddenly illumined by a flash of recollection; and starting up, she caught Henderson's hand.

But before she could speak he laid his fingers gently over her eyes.

"You are not to think," he said. "Tonight is past."

"But Hellier Crescent? What happened after — after — ?"

Again he made a soothing movement.

"You must not think of it. They gathered round me. They were generous. They heaped coals of fire."

Enid lay silent, conscious with a keen yet poignant pleasure of his hand upon her face. Then suddenly a new thought obtruded itself, and drawing away his fingers, she looked up into his face.

"And after tonight — ?" she said, in a low, unsteady voice.

For a moment he did not answer, and in the soft light it seemed to her that a shadow of pain passed over his face.

Again she put out her hand and touched his.

"What are you going to do?" she asked, below her breath.

At last he raised his head and looked fully at her.

"I am going back to the East. The hardest task of my life is awaiting me there. It is a very bitter thing to disillusionize the person to whom one is a hero."

She looked at him quickly.

"You are speaking of your mother? You are thinking of your mother?"

He bent his head.

For a space neither spoke. Vaguely, and in distant accompaniment to their thoughts, each was conscious of the hum of traffic and of the softly crackling fire; then at last Enid stirred, and with a gesture full of comprehension, her fingers closed round Henderson's.

"Let me tell her the story!" she said, almost inaudibly. "Take

me with you — and let me tell her! We are both women, and —"
Her head drooped slightly; and her face flushed. "And we both
love you."

THE END

www.ingramcontent.com/pod-product-compliance
Lightning Source LLC
Chambersburg PA
CBHW030540180626
46810CB00005B/1942